# Trial and Terror

The Hardys ran up the stairs to the roof, but there was no sign of the mysterious figure they were following. Below, streetlamps and apartment windows shone with light, but up on the roof it was pitch dark. The buildings on the block were crammed up against one another, and Frank realized the person could get to the end of the block merely by running along the rooftops.

"This certainly makes New York a convenient place for burglars," Frank said to Joe. "Let's split up."

Joe went east, and Frank went west. Frank peered through the darkness as he moved along the asphalt. Soon he took a small step down onto the roof of a neighboring building.

Then there was a dark blur of motion, and Frank glimpsed a figure rushing toward him. Frank backpedaled, but the figure gave him a rough shove, which sent him staggering farther backward.

In a split second, Frank realized the worst possible thing was happening. He was toppling over the edge of the rooftop. . . .

# The Hardy Boys Mystery Stories

# Available from MINSTREL Books

# THE HARDY BOYS®

## 147

# TRIAL AND TERROR

## FRANKLIN W. DIXON

A MINSTREL® BOOK

Published by POCKET BOOKS
New York   London   Toronto   Sydney   Tokyo   Singapore

This book is a work of fiction. Names, characters, places and incidents are products of the author's imagination or are used fictitiously. Any resemblance to actual events or locales or persons, living or dead, is entirely coincidental.

A MINSTREL PAPERBACK *Original*

A Minstrel Book published by
POCKET BOOKS, a division of Simon & Schuster Inc.
1230 Avenue of the Americas, New York, NY 10020

Copyright © 1997 by Simon & Schuster Inc.

Front cover illustration by John Youssi

Produced by Mega-Books, Inc.

All rights reserved, including the right to reproduce this book or portions thereof in any form whatsoever. For information address Pocket Books, 1230 Avenue of the Americas, New York, NY 10020

ISBN: 0-671-00059-4

First Minstrel Books printing December 1997

10  9  8  7  6  5  4  3  2  1

THE HARDY BOYS MYSTERY STORIES is a trademark of Simon & Schuster Inc.

THE HARDY BOYS, A MINSTREL BOOK and colophon are registered trademarks of Simon & Schuster Inc.

Printed in the U.S.A.

# Contents

# TRIAL AND TERROR

# 1 What Happened on the Night of August 14?

"I wonder what this trial is all about," Joe Hardy said as he and his brother, Frank, took seats in the spectator gallery of a criminal courtroom. A trial was about to continue after a lunchtime break, and the room buzzed with excitement.

"Keep a lid on, little bro'," Frank said, "and we'll soon find out."

Frank had volunteered to observe some court trials as part of a civics class project. Since he was doing the assignment over the Christmas break, Frank decided to watch some trials in New York City, which was just an hour's drive from the Hardys' hometown of Bayport. Frank knew the city would offer a greater variety of cases.

When Joe heard that Frank was going to observe actual trials, he invited himself along.

1

Frank and Joe had spent the morning looking in on several different cases. They could see that this courtroom was far more crowded than the others. By now almost every seat in the spectator gallery was taken.

"Let's see," Joe said. "So far today, we've seen trials involving burglary, embezzlement, and shoplifting. You know what we need now?"

"What's that?" Frank asked.

"A good murder trial," Joe said.

"I think we're in luck," Frank said, his brown eyes twinkling.

Tall and dark-haired, Frank was eighteen years old. He was in excellent physical shape, but he prided himself more on his brain power.

Blond-haired Joe was an inch shorter and a year younger than his brother. Joe often found himself guided more by his emotions and his muscle power than by logic and reason.

"Okay, let's get this show on the road," Joe said now, glancing around impatiently. He could see two men with their backs to the spectators, sitting at a long table. One of them, a man in his late twenties, turned around and glanced at Joe, almost as if he had heard what Joe had said. He was dressed in a blue suit, and his black hair was slicked back. Though his face seemed kind, his nervousness indicated to Joe that he was the person on trial.

"The defendant doesn't look like a murderer," Joe said to Frank.

Frank studied the man. "Time will tell, I guess."

Just then, one of the court officers, who the Hardys knew from the morning's proceedings was called a bailiff, stepped forward and called out, "All rise!"

Everyone stood as the judge, a distinguished-looking man dressed in a black robe, entered the room. He took a seat behind a massive desk that was elevated off the floor. Everyone sat back down.

"Miss Daggett, you may proceed with your case," the judge announced in a deep voice.

A tall woman whom Frank guessed was in her forties stood at another long table. She wore an elegant outfit, and every strand of her frosted blond hair was in place. Frank realized Daggett was the prosecuting lawyer, the person who would try to send the defendant to prison.

Frank couldn't tell how long the trial had been going, but he knew from civics class the general procedure the trial would follow. First the prosecuting lawyer would call a series of witnesses whose testimony would indicate the defendant's guilt. Then the defense lawyer would call witnesses whose testimony would indicate the defendant's innocence. The two lawyers were like warriors, each struggling to win victory over the other.

"Your Honor," Daggett said in a firm voice, "the prosecution calls Karen Lee to the stand."

All eyes watched Karen Lee enter the courtroom and walk to the witness stand. She was a pretty woman whom Joe guessed to be in her late twenties. Silky black hair grazed the shoulders of her dress.

A bailiff approached Lee and instructed her to raise her right hand. When Lee did so, the bailiff said, "Do you swear to tell the truth, the whole truth, and nothing but the truth?"

"I do," Karen Lee said. Joe thought she seemed calm and collected but not very happy to be there.

Daggett began by asking Lee some questions about who she was. Lee explained that for several years she had been a struggling actress, taking all sorts of odd jobs to make money. Then earlier this year, she had landed a role on a soap opera called *Days of Destiny.*

"That might explain why there are so many people here," Joe whispered to Frank. "People come out of the woodwork to see a celebrity."

Then Daggett got down to business. "Miss Lee," she said, walking toward the witness, "let me take you back to the night of August fourteenth of this year. Could you please tell the court what you were doing at approximately eight o'clock on that night?"

"Yes. Nick Rodriguez came by my apartment to talk with me," Lee replied.

"And what was your relationship with Nick Rodriguez?" Daggett asked.

4

"We were engaged to be married, but we had broken up two months before," Lee said. She paused. "Actually, I had broken up with Nick, and he was upset about it. That's what he wanted to talk to me about."

"Is Nick Rodriguez in this courtroom?" Daggett said. "And, if so, could you point him out?"

Karen Lee hesitated a moment. Then Joe watched her point at the defendant. "That's him in the blue suit," Lee said softly.

Daggett looked at the defendant, her eyes cold as ice. Then she turned back to Lee and asked, "How did your talk with Mr. Rodriguez go?"

"Not so well," Lee said. "We ended up arguing, and Nick left around nine o'clock."

"Was he distraught at the time?" Daggett said.

"Yes, he was," Lee answered.

"Did he have anything with him?" Daggett said.

"He had a large shopping bag," Lee said. "He told me he had been to a department store to buy some towels for his home."

Joe saw the defendant, Nick Rodriguez, shifting uneasily in his chair. The defense lawyer scribbled a note on his legal pad.

"Then what happened after Mr. Rodriguez left your apartment?" Daggett asked.

Lee cleared her throat. "A few minutes later," she said, "there was a knock at my door. When I opened it, I saw a person in disguise."

Until now spectators had been rustling and whispering, but now the courtroom fell silent.

"What kind of disguise?" Daggett asked.

"The person wore a long black coat and black gloves, and the face was completely covered by a black ski mask," Lee answered.

Frank kept his eyes glued to the witness, trying to see if anything in her manner would let him know if she was telling the truth.

"What happened next?" Daggett asked.

Lee cleared her throat again. "The person pushed me aside, got into the apartment, and closed the door behind," she said. "I tried to scream, but I was so frightened that nothing came out of my mouth. Then the intruder pulled a long knife from a coat pocket and lunged at me, the knife in the person's right hand."

Lee touched her throat and closed her eyes, almost as if she were reliving the moment.

"Take your time, Miss Lee," Daggett said. "I realize this is very difficult for you."

Lee took a deep breath, then continued. "I grabbed the hand just before the blade reached my chest. I held the hand tightly, struggling to get control of the knife, but finally the other person managed to pull it away. Again the knife came at me. Again I tried to scream, and this time I screamed really loud. When I did this, the person in black fled the apartment."

"Then what happened?" Daggett asked.

"I called the police," Lee said. "And some of

my neighbors came to my door. But none of them had caught a glimpse of the person in black."

Daggett paused to let the story sink in.

"It's not a murder case," Joe said to Frank, "but at least it's an *attempted* murder case."

Frank looked to the side of the courtroom where the jury was sitting in two rows behind a railing. After both lawyers had presented their cases, it would be the jury's job to decide if this man, Nick Rodriguez, was guilty or not guilty of attempting to murder Karen Lee.

Daggett questioned Lee for another few minutes before returning to her chair. Then the judge told the defense lawyer, a man named Myers, to begin his cross-examination.

Frank leaned forward. He knew that after one side questioned a witness, the other side always got a chance to ask some questions of its own.

Myers stood, hands in his pockets. Frank guessed he was in his early thirties. His rumpled suit and tousled hair made him seem an unworthy opponent to the elegant Daggett.

"Miss Lee, how are you this afternoon?" Myers asked. He was acting friendly, but Frank knew he would now try to cast doubt on Lee's testimony.

"I'm fine, thank you," Lee said, calm again.

"You say this person who attacked you on the night of August fourteenth was wearing a long coat and gloves, and the person's face was completely covered by a ski mask," Myers said. "Is that correct?"

"Yes, it is," Lee said.

"In other words," Myers said, "you really couldn't see this person at all."

"I guess not," Lee admitted. Frank noticed Lee crossing her legs, looking a little uncomfortable now.

"How tall was this person?" Myers asked.

"Average height," Lee answered.

"Average height," Myers said, as if thinking deeply about this. "What does that mean exactly? Somewhere between three and eight feet tall."

There was a ripple of laughter in the room. "Between five foot six inches and five foot ten inches, I would say," Lee answered. "I was flustered at the time."

"I'm sure you were," Myers said with a sympathetic nod. "In fact, you were probably so flustered you wouldn't be able to describe this person's weight or posture or shoe size or really any physical detail. Is that correct?"

"I suppose it is," Lee said, nervously touching a hand to her hair.

Myers pulled off a pair of glasses and looked at Lee. "Miss Lee," he said, "can you say with absolute certainty that the person who attacked you on the night of August fourteenth was Nick Rodriguez?"

"No," Lee said. "Not with absolute certainty."

"Oh, come on," Joe whispered to Frank. "It

seems pretty obvious Rodriguez is guilty, doesn't it? The knife and disguise were in the shopping bag, probably buried under the towels he said he had. He had decided if she didn't get back together with him, he was going to kill her."

"There might be a lot more to the story," Frank said, never one to jump to conclusions. "The testimony only proves that someone attacked Lee—not *who* attacked her."

After a few more questions, Lee was dismissed. Then Frank watched as Daggett called a police detective to the witness stand. The detective told how he and his partner went to Lee's apartment shortly after the attack. After questioning Lee and collecting some physical evidence, the two cops went to Nick Rodriguez's apartment.

Rodriguez was already home, the officer explained. He insisted he was innocent and showed the cops the towels he had bought, along with the receipt for them. The cops left. However, they went back to Rodriguez's apartment the following afternoon with a search warrant. This time they found a black ski mask and a pair of black gloves stuffed under the mattress in Rodriguez's bedroom. Rodriguez was then arrested.

"Man, he's looking guiltier by the minute, isn't he?" Joe whispered to Frank.

"Looks that way," Frank said. "But we can't jump to conclusions."

Myers briefly cross-examined the cop, then the

9

cop was dismissed. Daggett's next witness was a thin man named Roth. Joe thought Roth looked bored, as if he had done this many times.

"Mr. Roth, what is your occupation?" Daggett asked the man.

"I work in the police crime lab," Roth said. "My job is to evaluate physical evidence in New York City criminal cases."

"Have you examined the ski mask and gloves found in Nick Rodriguez's apartment?" Daggett said. Frank saw she was twirling a ring on her finger.

"Yes," Roth answered.

"What did you find?" Daggett asked.

"I found nothing useful in the gloves," Roth replied. "But I found several hair samples in the ski mask. We analyzed them, then got some samples of Nick Rodriguez's hair and compared them."

"Did the hair samples you found match with the samples taken from Nick Rodriguez?" Daggett asked.

"In my opinion, they did," Roth said as he straightened his tie. "All of them."

"What does that mean exactly?" Daggett asked.

"Every person's hair is different if you analyze it under a microscope," Roth explained. "Hair samples, in my opinion, can be matched with almost as much accuracy as fingerprints."

"What are the odds the hairs found in the ski

10

mask are *not* from Nick Rodriguez?" Daggett asked.

"Those hair samples belong to Nick Rodriguez," Roth said, glancing at the defendant. "I would say the odds against it are a million to one."

Excited voices passed through the courtroom, and the judge banged his gavel for order.

"Are you convinced he's guilty now?" Joe said.

"Just about," Frank replied.

Then a young woman in the front row of the gallery stood up and cried to the crowd, "No! He's innocent! I swear to you, he's innocent!"

# 2 Free PI Service

One of the bailiffs hurried over to the woman. Everyone turned to watch, and suddenly the room was alive with excited chatter.

"Order in the court!" the judge boomed, banging his gavel on his desk. "Order in the court!" The crowd quieted down as the bailiff escorted the young woman out of the courtroom.

"Ladies and gentlemen," the judge warned, "any more outbursts like that, and I will clear this room of all spectators. This is a court of law, not a circus. Now let us continue with the testimony."

"Let's go check on that woman," Frank whispered to Joe. "I want to see if she's all right."

"Good idea," Joe said, grabbing his coat.

The Hardys slipped out of the courtroom and

entered the corridor outside. Frank saw the bailiff had brought a chair and a glass of water to the young woman. As the bailiff returned to the courtroom, the woman sat in the chair, holding the water and staring blankly into space.

Frank and Joe approached the woman. "Are you okay, ma'am?" Frank asked.

"I'm not sure," the woman said quietly.

"Is there anything we can do?" Joe said.

"This is just very hard for me," the woman said, looking up at the Hardys. "That's my twin brother on trial, and I know he didn't do it."

Frank could see how much the woman resembled Nick Rodriguez. She was the same age, with the same features and the same coloring. She was an attractive woman, but sadness now filled her eyes.

"I'm Frank Hardy," Frank said gently, "and this is my brother, Joe. I'm here watching some trials for a school civics class."

"Hello," the woman said, managing a small smile. "My name is Nellie Rodriguez."

"If your brother is innocent," Joe said, "I'm sure his lawyer will get the jury to see that."

"But the evidence is all against him," Nellie said with a helpless shrug. "When that man talked about the hair samples, I could see every member of that jury convicting Nick with their eyes."

13

There was a blinding flash of light, and Joe turned to see a woman with frizzy red hair pointing a camera at Nellie. The woman was in her thirties, dressed in a turtleneck sweater and short leather skirt.

"Miss Rodriguez," the redhead spoke out, "I wonder if I might have a few words with you?"

"No," Nellie said angrily. "I've told you before, I have nothing to say to you. Please, can't you leave me and my family in peace?"

"It will only take—" the woman persisted.

"Can't you see she's upset?" Joe barked at the intruder. "Now get out of here!"

"Okay, okay, I'm going," the redhead said as she stuffed the camera into her large shoulder bag and hurried back to the courtroom.

"That's Lisa Velloni," Nellie said. Joe could tell that Nellie disliked the woman. "She's a reporter. Several newspapers, mostly tabloids, are covering this case because Karen is on a soap opera."

Nellie took a sip of water, then spoke again. "I'm told Patricia Daggett seldom loses a case. And she's prosecuting this one especially hard."

"Why is that?" Joe asked.

"Before she landed her TV role, Karen Lee worked as a secretary in the district attorney's office," Nellie explained. "That's where all the

14

prosecutors work. She was only there a few
months, but during that time Daggett and Lee
got to know each other. That gives Daggett all
the more reason to nail the person who tried to
kill Karen."

"Daggett's tough," Frank said, "but it seems as
if your brother's lawyer is also good."

"Bernie Myers is doing his best," Nellie said,
"but he's not even sure my brother is innocent.
Nick swears he had never seen those gloves and
ski mask before, let alone put them under the
mattress. But it sure looks like he did."

"Maybe your brother was framed," Frank said.

"That's exactly what I think," Nellie said.

"Do you know of anyone who might want to
kill Karen Lee?" Joe asked.

"That's part of the problem," Nellie said.
"Karen Lee is a very nice person who doesn't
seem to have any enemies. Aside from Nick,
there simply isn't anyone else with a motive to
kill her."

"Let me ask you something," Frank said.
"Does Mr. Myers have a private investigator
working on the case?"

"He suggested we hire one," Nellie said, "but
we couldn't afford it. We couldn't even afford to
put up Nick's bail money, so he's had to stay in
jail since his arrest."

Frank did not know if Nick Rodriguez was
guilty or innocent, but, either way, he felt great

15

sympathy for Nellie Rodriguez. She seemed like a nice person who was caught in a very painful situation. Frank gave his brother a look, and Joe gave a slight nod.

"Nellie," Frank said, kneeling beside the woman, "my brother and I do some detective work ourselves. Maybe we could lend a hand on this case."

"I'll bet we've got a record as good as Patricia Daggett's," Joe said proudly.

"It's very nice of you to offer, but . . ." Nellie began, doubt in her eyes.

"And we're cheap," Joe said. "In fact, we're free."

"Free?" Nellie asked, now clearly confused. "Nothing's free. What's the catch?"

"We take on cases because they interest us or because we want to help someone," Frank explained.

"Or both," Joe added.

"Well, I . . ." Nellie said.

"I have an idea," Frank said. "We'll do a little preliminary investigating today, and then we'll give Mr. Myers a report. If he doesn't like what we're doing, he doesn't have to use us."

"I guess we've got nothing to lose," Nellie said.

"Nothing at all," Joe said, a twinkle in his blue eyes.

Nellie gave the Hardys some more information

16

on Karen Lee, including her home address. Then she told the brothers to come back to the courthouse at five-fifteen, when they could talk with Mr. Myers.

The Hardys rode the elevator down to the lobby, then walked to the bottom of the building's concrete steps. The winter air was brisk but not too cold. After being inside stuffy courtrooms all day, Joe found the air refreshing.

"I don't know if we'll be able to help on this case," Joe said, stretching his arms, "but at least you'll get a great report for your civics class."

"This should be interesting," Frank said. "We've never worked as PIs on a trial before."

"And here we are," Joe said, "first time out, smack in the middle of an attempted murder case."

A steady flow of people moved up and down the steps. The criminal court building was a grimy granite structure that ascended twenty stories high. A large percentage of the criminal trials for the Manhattan borough of New York City took place there, and that added up to plenty of trial activity every day. Frank noticed a phrase engraved on a stone wall bordering the steps: Justice Denied No One.

"One thing I learned in civics class is that because this is a trial case," Frank told Joe, "we don't have to prove someone else is guilty. We

17

don't even have to prove Rodriguez is innocent. We just have to find things that will keep the jury from being absolutely certain he's the person who attacked Karen Lee. If even one of the jurors has some doubt about Rodriguez being the culprit, the jury has to let him go."

"I knew that," Joe said. "The Constitution says that a man is innocent until *proven* guilty."

"You're definitely going to get an A when you take civics next year as a senior," Frank said with a sly look. "And it will all be thanks to me, of course."

"Of course," Joe said, ignoring his brother's teasing. "I guess the best way for us to give the jury some reason to doubt would be to find a few other suspects."

"I was thinking we could first go to Karen Lee's apartment building," Frank said. "Maybe we'll find someone there who knows a little about her or who may have seen something useful on the night of August fourteenth."

"Sounds good," Joe said, already on the move.

The Hardys walked a few blocks to an outdoor parking lot. After paying an attendant, they climbed inside their trusty blue van, and Frank turned the key in the ignition.

Though it was only three o'clock, the streets heading uptown were clogged with cars, taxis, trucks, buses, and even bicycles. A mixture of honking horns and rumbling engines filled the air.

Looking out the back window of the van, Joe caught sight of the two sleek towers of the World Trade Center. Up ahead he picked out the familiar shape of the Empire State Building.

"With just a turn of the head, ladies and gentlemen," Joe said, mimicking the voice of a tour guide, "you can see the world's third and fourth tallest skyscrapers."

Without warning, a bright yellow taxi swerved in front of the van, forcing Frank to slam on his brakes. Then a chorus of angry horns blared from behind. "Man, this traffic is murder," Frank said.

"Welcome to New York City," Joe cracked.

After twenty minutes, the Hardys reached a neighborhood known as Chelsea. After another twenty minutes spent searching for a parking space, Frank and Joe were finally walking down the block where Karen Lee lived.

Chelsea was a residential area, much quieter than most of Manhattan. Small apartment houses stood on both sides of the tree-lined streets. Soon the Hardys found a five-story red-brick building that had the address they were looking for.

Frank and Joe climbed the front steps, and Frank tried the front door. It was locked. But when a postman stepped out of the building, the brothers were able to slip inside.

"Easy as pie," Joe said.

The building was clean and the hallways freshly painted. The Hardys passed an elevator and went through a door into a stairwell. After climbing two flights, they emerged through another door onto the third floor. There was a hallway that showed the doors to three apartments.

"Karen lives in three-C," Frank said, moving down the hallway. "Let's hope some of her neighbors are home, and let's hope they're the nosy type."

"Look," Joe said, pointing to a door that was slightly ajar. A small plaque on the door read 3C.

Frank knocked on the door. When there was no answer, he and Joe stepped quietly inside.

They were in a living room. The lights were off, and there was no sign of anyone around. Frank noticed it seemed almost colder indoors than outside. It's the middle of December, Frank thought. Why is the building's heat not on?

Joe moved to a desk upon which everything was neatly arranged. A large manila envelope was open, and numerous smaller envelopes were sticking out of it. All the envelopes were addressed to Karen Lee, care of the *Days of Destiny* television studio. Fan letters, Joe thought.

Meanwhile Frank was moving down a hallway that he guessed led to a bedroom and a bathroom. Then Frank stopped, his heart pounding.

The bathroom light was on, and inside, half under the sink, Frank saw a body sprawled on the bathroom floor.

# 3 Garbage

Frank crept down the hallway and into the bathroom. When he reached the bathroom door, he let out an audible sigh. A young man was lying on his back, his head under the sink, just as Frank had seen. But the man was quite alive, and he held a pipe wrench in one hand.

"Who are you?" the man said, lifting his head to look at Frank. He was somewhere in his mid-twenties, dressed in blue jeans and a flannel shirt. He had a dramatic-looking face, Frank thought. The hair was dark, the nose sharp, and the eyes intense, like those of a falcon.

"I'm sorry for barging in, but the door was open," Frank said. He could see the man was in the middle of changing a pipe.

"I'll say it again," the man said, eyeing Frank suspiciously. "Who are you?"

Joe appeared at Frank's side. "I'm Frank Hardy," Frank said, "and this is my brother, Joe. We're doing some research on the Karen Lee trial as part of a high school journalism assignment. We thought we would just take a look at her building. But then we found the door to her apartment open."

Frank and Joe looked, dressed, and acted like two ordinary high school kids, and it often worked to their advantage if people thought they were nothing more than that.

"So you guys are aspiring writers?" the man asked, looking from Frank to Joe.

"You might say that," Frank replied. "We especially like nonfiction and love to do hands-on research."

The man chuckled, his suspicion quickly turning into friendliness. "Well, I'm the building's superintendent," he said, picking up a piece of shiny pipe. "When something breaks, I fix it. But I'm also a writer myself. The name's Alex Steel."

"What sort of stuff do you write?" Frank asked, pleased to see Alex was buying the phony journalism story.

"Murder mysteries," Alex said with a gleam in his eye. *"Death in the Living Room, What the Blind Man Saw, Blood Is My Favorite Color."*

"I've never heard of them," Joe said. "Sorry."

"That's okay. Nothing's been published yet," Alex said. "That's why I have the super job. I get some money, a free apartment, and the hours are short enough so I have plenty of time to work on my books."

"Do you know much about what happened to Karen Lee?" Frank asked.

"A little," Alex said, sliding back under the sink to continue his work. "I was in my apartment writing that night. I was in the middle of a scene in which a woman is moving through a dark basement. She has the feeling someone is in there, hiding in the shadows. Then I heard this bloodcurdling scream come from upstairs."

"You must have jumped," Joe said.

"Boy, did I," Alex said, wrapping a strip of string around the pipe. "I ran upstairs and found several people already in Karen's apartment."

"Did you see anyone leaving the building right around then?" Frank asked.

"No," Alex said, inserting the pipe under the sink. "I didn't hear the elevator in use or see anyone on the steps. I think the attacker left through a hatchway to the roof, because later I noticed the hatch was left open."

"The attacker could have run to another rooftop and then come down a fire escape," Joe said.

"That's probably what happened," Alex said, turning the pipe in place with the wrench.

"Are you friendly with Karen?" Frank asked.

"We talk now and then," Alex replied. "She's

interested in my stories, and I'm interested in her acting career. Fellow artists, you know."

"Aside from Rodriguez, do you know of anyone who would have reason to kill her?" Joe said.

"I can't say I do," Alex said, grunting as he gave the pipe a final turn. "Karen Lee is one of the kindest people I've ever met. I can't imagine anybody would be out to get her."

Finished with the pipe, Alex dropped the wrench into a plastic bucket filled with tools. When he stood up, Frank noticed he was tall and well built. "Okay, Frank and Joe," Alex said, lifting the bucket. "I can't let you stay in here."

"It's cold in this building," Frank said as Alex escorted the Hardys down the hallway.

"Yeah, there's a problem with the thermostat," Alex explained. "Until I get a repairman in here, there's no heat. Everyone's been complaining."

When Alex and the Hardys stepped out of the apartment, Alex locked the door and pocketed the keys.

"Here's a phone number where you can reach us," Joe said, handing Alex a piece of paper. "If you think of anything that might fill in any details for us, please call."

Frank saw an elderly woman in a heavy coat standing at the door next to Lee's apartment. A knit cap covered most of her gray hair. She was rummaging through a purse, but she now looked up.

"Oh, Alex," the woman said. "I'm so glad you're here. I can't seem to find my apartment keys. Could you please lend me the set you have?"

"Sure thing, Mrs. Petrowski," Alex said with a wave. "I'll be right back with it."

Alex took the elevator down, but Frank and Joe stayed upstairs, hoping to get some information from Mrs. Petrowski.

After giving her the same cover story they had told Alex, Joe said, "Mrs. Petrowski, do you remember anything about the night Karen was attacked?"

"I certainly do," Mrs. Petrowski said, clearly eager to be of help to the nice-looking high school students. "I saw Nick Rodriguez leaving Karen's apartment around nine. I was just coming home from my Tuesday evening bridge game. Then I went into my apartment. I was just about to turn on the TV to watch that police show with that actor who's so good."

"And then . . ." Joe prompted.

"Then I heard a scream that made me jump out of my skin," Mrs. Petrowski said. "I realized the scream must have come from Karen's place. Several of us rushed right over there, but none of us saw the man in black she told us about."

"Do you know of anyone who may have had reason to harm Karen Lee?" Frank asked.

"I certainly don't," Mrs. Petrowski said. "She's

26

the sweetest young woman in the world. Why, if it weren't for Karen, I might not have a home."

"Why do you say that?" Joe asked.

Mrs. Petrowski thought a moment, then spoke in a lower voice. "Well, some of the tenants in this building are older, like myself, and we've lived here a long time. And because of the city rent laws, our rents are low. But the building's landlord is trying to evict all us old folks so he can renovate our apartments. That will allow him to bring in new tenants and charge much higher rents."

"What does Karen Lee have to do with this?" Frank asked, his interest increasing.

"You see," Mrs. Petrowski said, shivering inside her heavy coat, "Karen used to work in the district attorney's office, and she knows something about the law. So she organized us seniors and filed motions in court to stop Mr. Garfein, the landlord, from evicting us."

When she heard the mechanical sound of the elevator returning to the third floor, Mrs. Petrowski stopped her story. "I hear Alex coming," she whispered to the Hardys. "Do me a favor. Don't tell him I was talking about Mr. Garfein."

"Why not?" Joe whispered back.

"Alex isn't a bad fellow," Mrs. Petrowski said, "but he works for Mr. Garfein. I just don't want it getting back to Garfein that I was saying bad things about him. He might try to make things even more difficult for me."

27

"I take it Mr. Garfein isn't the nicest guy around," Frank said with a chuckle.

"Fred Garfein is as mean as Karen Lee is sweet," Mrs. Petrowski whispered.

"We won't say a word," Joe assured her.

The elevator doors opened, and Alex handed Mrs. Petrowski a set of keys. Not wanting to appear too inquisitive, the Hardys rode the elevator back down with Alex and left the building.

Outside, Frank and Joe sat on the building's stoop to collect their thoughts. The afternoon light was already fading, and the air was turning chillier. Joe watched two boys go in-line skating down the block.

"We may have our first suspect," Frank said.

"Who?" Joe asked. "Fred Garfein?"

"It sounds as if Karen Lee is the one stopping him from his renovation plans," Frank said, zipping up his coat. "I doubt a businessman like Garfein would do it himself, but he could have hired someone to scare Lee."

"It's possible. Remind me not to rent an apartment from Garfein when I'm out on my own," Joe said with a chuckle.

Joe noticed a young man in his early twenties sitting on a stoop across the street. He was a clean-cut guy with wire-rimmed glasses and a down ski vest.

Joe nudged Frank. "Hey, look. I remember seeing that guy at the trial."

"Hey!" Joe called out to the man. "Are you one of the reporters from the trial?"

The young man gave a nod. Joe gave him the thumbs-up sign.

"He must be waiting to ask Lee some questions when she comes home," Frank told Joe. "I'd like to ask her some questions myself."

"Like what?" Joe said.

"Well, if those gloves and ski mask didn't belong to Nick," Frank said, forming a thought, "then someone must have put them there. Someone who had access to Nick's apartment. So I'm wondering if Lee had keys to Nick's apartment that the culprit could have stolen."

"Hmm, worth checking out," Joe said, his eyes scanning the sidewalk in front of the building, where garbage cans were kept inside an iron railing. He noticed a man in ragged clothing searching through one of the cans. The man had a shopping cart filled with old clothing and cast-off appliances.

"That gives me an idea," Joe said, watching the man examine a soiled magazine. "Maybe I'll find some clues in Karen Lee's garbage. Letters or something. After all, it's one of the oldest detective tricks in the book."

Joe walked over to the garbage area, lifted the top off one of the rubber cans, and opened a small plastic bag to investigate its contents. He found lettuce, chicken bones, and some papers.

"Hey, what're you doing?" a voice cried.

Suddenly Joe felt hands grab him roughly by the shoulders and spin him around. Joe was looking into the wild-eyed face of a homeless man—who looked as if he would stop at nothing to protect his turf.

# 4 The Missing Keys

"Hey, buster," the homeless man growled in a gravelly voice. "This is my garbage! Understand? My garbage!"

"And this is a free country," Joe said, pulling away from the man's grasp. "Which means I have as much right to this garbage as you do!"

Joe and the man glared at each other while Frank trotted over. Seeing that it was about to be two against one, the man backed away.

"All right, all right—you win. But if you find any telephones or coffeepots or anything good like that, they're mine."

"Deal," Joe said, clapping the man's shoulder.

Minutes later Joe returned to the stoop carrying a small plastic bag filled with trash.

"Sniff out any good clues?" Frank joked.

"Make fun of me if you want to," Joe said, pulling out some soiled envelopes, "but these are letters addressed to Karen Lee. Can you think of a better way to learn about someone than by reading her mail?"

"Either that or by talking to her," Frank said, glancing up the block. "Look who's headed our way."

At that moment Karen Lee herself was walking toward the building.

"She must have left soon after her testimony," Joe said. "I guess she doesn't have to be there for the entire trial."

The Hardys stood as Lee approached the stoop. "Miss Lee," Frank said, "my brother and I are working on a high school journalism assignment, and I wonder if I could ask you a question or two."

When Karen Lee smiled, Frank could see why she had won a role on television. Not only was she pretty, but she seemed to radiate a glow of warmth.

"I'm not supposed to talk with anyone about the trial," Lee said politely. "But if it's just for a high school project, I guess it won't hurt."

Joe noticed the reporter across the street had stood when Lee approached. But oddly, Joe noticed, he made no move to approach.

"When you were engaged to Nick Rodriguez,"

Frank asked Lee, "did you have keys to his apartment? And, if so, were they labeled?"

Lee seemed surprised by the question. "Uh, well, yes, I did have keys to Nick's apartment," she said after a moment. "And, yes, there was a label with his first name on it."

"And I'm sorry to pry," Frank said, "but did you keep the keys after the two of you broke up?"

"I meant to give them back," Lee said, nervously pushing back her hair, "but I never did."

"Do you still have those keys?" Frank asked.

"I'm sorry, but I have to go," Lee said, starting up the stoop. "As I told you, I'm really not supposed to talk about any of this."

"Miss Lee," Frank said, his tone serious, "Nick Rodriguez is someone you once cared about. No matter what Patricia Daggett may have told you, isn't the truth more important than putting Nick behind bars?"

Lee met Frank's eyes. She wriggled her hands inside her coat pockets as if wrestling with a decision, then she seemed to give in.

"Shortly after the attack," she began, "I noticed the keys were missing. I probably just misplaced them. I told Miss Daggett about this, and if it were important, I'm sure she would have made this information available to the defense. Now, if you'll excuse me, I really do have to go."

"Thank you, Miss Lee," Frank said as Lee let herself into the apartment building.

"Good work," Joe told Frank. "She *did* have keys to Rodriguez's apartment."

"Right," Frank said. "At the very least, those missing keys show how someone could have planted the gloves and ski mask in Nick's place. It's not proof, but it's a possibility."

"Except," Joe said, warming his hands in his coat pocket, "according to Lee's testimony, the attacker wouldn't have had a chance to get the keys during the time of the attack. Which means they must have gotten the keys another time. Lee wouldn't give Nick's keys away. So how would this person have gotten them?"

"Alex, for one, has keys to Lee's apartment," Frank said. "We just saw him use them."

"He did seem to like those gory book titles," Joe said. "Remember *Death in the Living Room?* But could he have been the one who attacked Lee?"

"Sure. At this point, we can't rule anyone out," Frank said. "We have to consider every possible scenario."

"Let's see," Joe said, glancing back at the apartment house. "Lee's apartment is in the back of the building. As I recall, a fire escape runs right by her living room window. Since the crime happened in the summer, there's a chance that window might have been open. Which means that someone could have used the fire escape to get into Lee's apartment and find Nick's keys."

"And," Frank said, glancing at his watch,

34

"Nick's apartment could also have a fire escape leading to it. We should make a check on that. Come on, we need to get back down to the courthouse."

As dusk fell over the city, streetlamps and neon signs began glowing. Evening seemed to make the taxis bolder, with many of them cutting in and out of lanes as if they were in a Hollywood action movie. Frank held his own, though, eager to get downtown for the five-fifteen meeting with Myers.

While Frank drove, Joe occupied himself with looking through the bag of trash he had found.

"Enjoying that garbage?" Frank asked.

"Just you watch," Joe said. "This garbage is going to produce a valuable clue. I can just feel it."

"Or smell it," Frank replied with a chuckle.

Once downtown, Frank found a parking space on a side street, and the Hardys returned to the criminal court building. They soon found Nellie Rodriguez and Bernie Myers waiting in the gloomy corridor where the Hardys had spoken earlier with Nellie. Holding a briefcase, Myers looked even more rumpled than before.

"Nellie explained to me your very generous offer to help out," Myers said, rubbing his eyes beneath his glasses, "but I really don't think you boys are qualified for this kind of work."

Without taking offense, Frank and Joe explained what they had learned that afternoon about Fred Garfein's eviction plans and the missing set of keys.

Myers was silent a moment. "Well, I just did something a lawyer should never do," he said with a chuckle. "I spoke too soon. I take back my previous statement. In a few short hours, you boys have done some excellent work."

"And you haven't even heard about the garbage yet," Frank said with a sly glance at Joe.

"However," Myers continued, "if I'm going to imply to the jury that someone else committed this crime, I'm going to need a bit more evidence to back up my claim. What you have now isn't quite strong enough for me to bring into the courtroom."

"We're on it," Joe said.

"You don't have long," Myers pointed out. "The prosecution rested its case this afternoon. I start my defense tomorrow morning, and I guess it will take about two days. Today is Monday. If you're going to find something usable, I need to have it by Wednesday afternoon."

"Two things," Frank told Myers. "First, could we get keys to Nick's apartment? We want to check ways someone might have gotten in there. Second, would it be possible for us to look at the evidence the police collected from the scene of the crime?"

"I've already checked the evidence," Myers said. "There's really nothing helpful there."

"With all due respect, sir," Frank said, "we

might find something you may have overlooked. You're a lawyer, and we're detectives."

Myers looked the Hardys up and down. "Okay," he said with a nod. "I've got the keys in my briefcase, and tomorrow I'll request permission for you to look at the evidence. Right now Nellie and I are going to visit Nick. Why don't you guys come along?"

"That would be great, Mr. Myers," Frank said.

"And by the way," Myers told the Hardys, "call me Bernie."

"You two are doing a wonderful job," Nellie said, her face beaming with approval.

The group left the courthouse and walked to the Manhattan House of Detention, a high-rise building next door. On the tenth floor a policeman took the Hardys, Nellie, and Myers into one of the interview rooms in which defendants were allowed to meet with their lawyers.

Everyone sat at a table under a harsh fluorescent light. "Nick has been in this place since his arrest, right?" Joe asked.

"I'm afraid so," Myers said. "If defendants can't afford bail, they have to stay here until their trial comes up. And for serious crimes, the bail can be a lot of money. Nick's been here four months."

Joe knew the bail was to ensure that the defendant would show up for the trial rather than avoid it. If they did show up, the money was returned.

37

Soon a policeman brought in Nick Rodriguez, who was now dressed in gray prison overalls. Nick took a seat at the table, and Myers introduced him to the Hardys.

"Thanks for your help," Nick told the Hardys as he shook their hands.

He was a handsome man up close, Frank thought. Even so, Frank could see the strain of the trial in Nick's face. Wanting to learn more about Karen Lee, Frank asked Nick to talk a bit about his relationship with her.

"I first met Karen two years ago," Nick said, his hands resting on the table in front of him. "She came into the computer software store where I work, and we seemed to hit it off. I worked up the nerve to ask her out, and, to my amazement, she agreed."

"And you dated for a while, right?" Frank asked.

Nick nodded. "And we were happy," he said. "Every time we got together, it was like magic. After a year of dating, I asked her to marry me, and, again to my amazement, she accepted. This was last April."

"Then what happened?" Joe asked.

"A month later, in May," Nick said, "Karen finally got her big break. She landed a role on the soap opera *Days of Destiny*. Right away she was making pretty good money, and people were recognizing her everywhere we went."

"Is that what came between you?" Frank

asked. "The fact that her career was taking off and you still had the same job in a computer store?"

Nick let out a heavy breath. "I'm not sure what came first," he said. "Me being jealous of the glamor in her life or her becoming distant. It was probably a little of both. Suddenly . . . I don't know . . . the magic vanished."

"Then she broke up with you," Joe said.

"Yeah. It was a beautiful day in June," Nick said, a far-off look in his eyes. "We were walking through Central Park. She said her feelings for me were cooling off a bit, and it would be a big mistake for us to get married. She slipped off the diamond ring I had given her and handed it back to me."

Nick paused a moment. Frank was watching him carefully, trying to determine if this man was guilty or innocent. Out of the corner of his eye, he could see Joe was doing the same thing.

"I told her I'd try harder," Nick continued. "I'd be nicer, more supportive—anything she wanted. But she said no, and that her decision was final."

"Then what happened between you?" Frank asked.

"I moped around a few days, then I started trying to get back together with her," Nick explained. "I called every week or so, but nothing I could say would change her mind. That's why I went to see her on the night of August fourteenth. I wanted to try to win her back one last time. Face-to-face."

"But it didn't work," Joe said quietly.

Nick shook his head sadly. "This was such a hard time for me," he said. "I was feeling so many bad things. Anger, rejection, loneliness. I felt lost."

"But you wouldn't hurt her, would you?" Frank said, trying to get inside the man's mind.

"No!" Nick cried out, driving his fist down hard on the table, his dark eyes seething with rage. "I would never have hurt her! Don't you see? I was in love with her!"

Joe jumped at this sudden outburst. He felt as if he had just witnessed an explosion.

At that moment Joe felt he was sitting across the table from a possible murderer.

# 5 A Foreboding Fortune

No one spoke for a moment.

"I'm sorry," Nick said finally, a surprised look on his face. "I'm not sure where that came from."

"It's all right, Nick," Myers said evenly. "You're under a lot of pressure these days."

"We're all on your side," Nellie said, taking her brother's hand.

Frank nodded his agreement, but he could see that Joe was not sure whose side he was on.

Staring at the table, Nick spoke in a calmer voice. "Do you have any idea what it's like for an innocent man to go through this? First the policemen came into my apartment and handcuffed me. Then they drove me downtown and took away my wallet, my keys, even my pocket change. Then they took mug shots of me and fingerprinted me. Then they locked me up behind bars like an animal in a cage."

As if showing how trapped he felt, Nick stood and walked across the room. He pounded the wall once, then said, "And you know what the worst part of this whole thing is? The very worst!"

"What, Nick?" Nellie asked.

Nick turned back to face the others. "The worst thing is that Karen believes I tried to kill her. I give you my solemn word—I did *not* try to kill her. And that is the truth!"

Nick returned to the table and sank into his chair, his head in his hands.

"Nick, do you know of anyone who might have done it?" Frank asked.

"No," Nick said, looking Frank squarely in the eye. "But there's one thing I do remember. When I left Karen's apartment that night, I walked down the hall and pushed the button for the elevator. And while I was standing there waiting, I glanced over at the door that leads to the stairwell. There's a small window in that door."

"I've seen it," Joe said, nodding.

"Well, for a second, I thought I saw a face in that window," Nick said. "At the time I didn't think anything of it, and I have no idea what the face looked like. But that was probably the real attacker. Whoever that might be."

"Will this be mentioned in court?" Frank asked, turning to Myers.

"Bernie won't say it," Nick cut in, "but the fact is, he's not sure he believes me about this face. You see, even Bernie thinks I did it!"

Myers sat silently in his chair, a finger to his lips, not arguing the point.

Soon the Hardys left to give Nellie and Myers some time alone with Nick. It was completely dark when Frank and Joe stepped out of the House of Detention, and they headed east in search of dinner.

After a few blocks, the Hardys found themselves in a maze of narrow, winding streets crowded with Chinese restaurants, shops, newsstands, and businesses.

The Hardys entered a small restaurant and sat at a table. A waiter brought the Hardys menus, chopsticks, and cups of steaming tea.

"You know," Joe said, opening his menu, "I still think Nick is guilty. Even more so now."

"That outburst was something," Frank said after a sip of tea. "But he's been cooped up for four months."

"That's true, but I think it really drove him crazy that he couldn't marry Karen Lee," Joe explained. "I think the anger just built up, day by day, and then on the night of August fourteenth the dam burst wide open. I think that flash of temper we saw was just a sample of what this guy has stored inside."

43

Frank and Joe spent several minutes in silence while they studied their menus.

"I think he's innocent," Frank said after they had placed their orders.

"Why?" Joe asked.

"For one thing," Frank said, "I don't think that outburst was anger at Karen Lee. I think it was anger that everybody thinks he could have tried to murder her. I was watching him carefully. Each time he got the least bit mad, it was about that. For another thing, Nick's not dumb. If he really did commit that crime, he would have gotten rid of the gloves and ski mask instead of stuffing them under his mattress. The cops found those items a whole day after the attack."

"But he's not a criminal," Joe said. "Amateurs make stupid mistakes all the time."

The Hardys argued the point several minutes, then steaming plates of food came. Frank's dish had a variety of fresh-looking seafood, and Joe's contained items Joe had never seen before.

"Well, guilty or not," Frank said, spearing a shrimp with his chopsticks, "everyone has a right to a fair trial."

"I guess that's why Bernie is doing his best to defend his client," Joe said, picking up a squiggly thing with his chopsticks. "Even though it seems he doesn't believe his client is innocent."

"Happens all the time," Frank said. "Hey, this is pretty decent chow."

"Do you think Bernie will put Nick on the witness stand?" Joe asked. "You know, give Nick a chance to tell his side of the story?"

"If Bernie thinks Nick is guilty, he probably won't," Frank replied. "He'll be afraid that Daggett will shake Nick up on the cross-examination and get the truth out of him."

While he ate, Joe mulled over the way the American criminal justice system worked. Was it right for him to help Nick's side of the case when he had a strong suspicion the man was guilty of a serious crime?

"I know what you're thinking," Frank said, watching his brother. "But remember, the reason defendants are supposed to get a fair trial is because a person is considered innocent until proven guilty. You said it yourself this afternoon."

Joe continued chewing and thinking. "Okay," he said, suddenly pulling some envelopes and papers from his coat. "I say we do our best for Nick Rodriguez."

"What are those?" Frank asked.

"The letters I found in Lee's trash," Joe said, spreading them out for a better look. "We've got to bring Bernie something good by the day after tomorrow, and I don't want to waste any time."

"So far we've got one possible suspect," Frank

45

said as Joe studied the envelopes. "Fred Garfein. I think we should pay him a visit first thing tomorrow and see what we can learn."

"Check this out," Joe said, sliding a piece of paper over to Frank. "It's a fan letter."

Frank looked at the letter. " 'Dear Karen,' " he read aloud. " 'I watch *Days of Destiny* every single day, and I've decided you are my favorite actress. In addition to being talented, you are also one of the most beautiful women on earth. This may sound strange, but somehow I feel we are fated to be together, and I hope one day this dream of mine will come true. That will be my Day of Destiny. I will be writing more letters to you in the near future.' Signed, 'John Q.' "

Frank finished reading and put the letter down.

"You know," Joe said, "a crazy fan could have attacked Karen Lee. It's been known to happen. And this guy goes a little overboard."

Frank studied the envelope. "Somehow this guy got Lee's home address," Frank said. "Which means he knows where she lives."

"And we know where he lives," Joe said, pointing to a return address on the envelope. It was a New York City address.

When the Hardys finished dinner, the waiter brought the check and two fortune cookies. Joe cracked open his cookie, pulled out a slip of paper, and read, " 'You make your family very proud.' "

46

"What a rip-off," Joe said, showing Frank the fortune. "Aren't these supposed to predict things?"

Frank cracked open his cookie and read the slip of paper. "Maybe you were expecting something more like this," he said, handing the paper to Joe.

The fortune read: Beware—you will find much danger in the big city.

"Yeah," Joe said. "I think something along those lines."

As Joe drove the van uptown, he saw as many people on the streets at night as he had in the daytime. They were in Times Square, the liveliest part of town at night. Several wide streets crisscrossed here, each of them jam-packed with theaters, shops, restaurants, video arcades, traffic, and plenty of people. Everywhere colored lights flashed and twinkled, and overhead gigantic advertising signs blazed big and bright.

"I bet there's enough electricity here to power Bayport for a month," Frank said, glancing around.

"This town is amazing," Joe declared as he stopped the van for a red light. "There's just so much of . . . well, everything."

"Especially people," Frank added. "I think about eight million people live here. And, boy, they've got every conceivable type."

"And out of all those people," Joe said, "we

have to find the one who attacked Karen Lee on the night of August fourteenth."

Traveling north for another ten minutes, the Hardys came to a quieter section of the city and parked on a residential block. After a short walk, they found the ten-story apartment building where Nick lived.

Using the keys Bernie gave them, the Hardys entered Nick's apartment, which was on the top floor. The place was messy, and Frank wondered if this was because the police had searched the apartment or because Nick was hauled off to jail without warning.

Frank and Joe looked out the living room windows and then did the same in the bedroom. "There's no fire escape directly leading to this apartment," Joe said when they were done. "If someone came in here to plant evidence, my guess is they had keys. They could have picked the locks, but not many people know how to do that. Present company excepted, of course."

"And this makes those missing keys look all the more suspicious," Frank said, glancing at the bed where the ski mask and gloves had been found. "That's good for the case. The culprit would—"

"Shhh," Joe said. "I think I heard something."

Frank briefly heard footsteps and then the front door of the apartment closing.

"Yep," Frank said, "that was definitely something. Somebody was just in the apartment."

The Hardys dashed into the living room and then out of the apartment. At the end of the hallway, they saw a door close. They rushed to the door, which opened into a stairwell, and heard footsteps clattering up the steps. As Frank and Joe ran up the steps, they heard a door above open, then slam shut.

"The roof," the two brothers said in unison, and they knew it meant only one thing—the person was getting away.

The Hardys passed through the second door. A blast of fresh air hit them, and they found themselves on the building's asphalt rooftop. Below, streetlamps and apartment windows shone with light, but up on the roof it was pitch dark.

Neither Frank nor Joe saw anyone around.

The buildings on the block were crammed up against one another, and Frank realized the person could get to the end of the block merely by running along the rooftops.

"This certainly makes New York a convenient place for burglars," he said to Joe. "Let's split up," he said, gesturing toward the river.

Joe went east, and Frank went west.

Frank peered through the darkness as he moved along the asphalt. Soon he took a small step down onto the roof of a neighboring building.

Then there was a dark blur of motion, and Frank glimpsed a figure rushing toward him.

Frank backpedaled, but the figure gave him a rough shove, which sent him staggering farther backward.

In a split second, Frank realized the worst possible thing was happening. He was toppling over the edge of the rooftop.

# 6 The Seventy-ninth Floor

Falling through empty space, Frank reached out for something—anything—to grab on to.

Frank's body jerked to a stop.

His right hand had grasped a rubber cable line that ran down the side of the building. Quickly Frank grabbed the line with his other hand, then he hung on for dear life. He could see he had grabbed the cable one story down from the roof. That meant the ground was still a good nine stories away.

"Joe!" Frank shouted. "Over here!"

Frank's heart was racing wildly, and he feared his brother would be out of hearing range by now, in search of the mysterious figure.

Then Frank felt the line slip. His weight was

too much. The line was pulling out of its connection to the roof.

Far below, Frank heard a car passing and a few people talking on the street. Even if someone down there could hear his call, Frank figured, they probably would not get to the roof in time.

The line slipped further.

Then Joe's blond head appeared over the side of the building. Joe reached for Frank but could not quite make it. Using his left hand, then right, then left again, Frank eased higher up the line.

"Gotcha!" Joe said, grabbing Frank's left wrist just before Frank plunged downward. Then, using the powerful muscles of his upper arms, Joe managed to haul his brother back up to the rooftop just as the line snapped.

"I think that fortune cookie is turning out to be right," Frank said, grateful to be on solid ground.

"What happened?" Joe asked.

"That person just sprang out of nowhere and gave me a good shove," Frank replied.

"What did the person look like?" Joe asked.

"I didn't get much of a look," Frank said, straining to remember the figure. "But I thought I saw some frizzy red hair sticking through a baseball cap. You know whose hair it looked like?"

"That pushy reporter we saw this afternoon?" Joe said. "She had frizzy red hair."

52

"Right," Frank said. "I think Nellie said her name was Lisa Velloni."

"Hmm, maybe she was snooping for information to help with her story," Joe figured.

"Maybe," Frank said. "But if it was her, how did she get in? And why was she so eager to get me out of the way? We should make a point of talking to her tomorrow."

Back at street level, the Hardys headed for the van, each brother lost in thought about the case. A siren whined on the avenue several blocks away.

"You know, I'm working up a theory about this guy John Q.," Joe said. "Let's assume he's obsessed with Karen Lee. He said he feels 'fated' to be with her. Maybe he learned she was engaged to Nick from one of those soap magazines or something, and maybe he never heard about them calling it off. Maybe it really burned him up that she was going to marry someone else."

"Even if he didn't know her?" Frank asked.

"People can get possessive about celebrities," Joe pointed out. "They think they know them just because they see them on TV all the time."

"So what are you saying?" Frank said. "That John Q. may have tried to kill Karen Lee?"

"Maybe he didn't intend to kill her," Joe said. "Maybe he just staged it to look that way."

"But why?" Frank asked.

"So he could frame Nick and get him out of the

picture," Joe said. "He planted the ski mask and gloves in Nick's apartment and got some strands of Nick's hair, say from a comb, and put them in the mask. Nick gets sent off to prison for a long time, and John Q. believes he can have Lee all to himself."

"Well, I guess it's possible," Frank said.

"And, remember, possibilities are all we need," Joe said. "So now we have two suspects to pursue. Fred Garfein and John Q. Not bad for a day's work."

"But, like Bernie told us," Frank said, "we still have to find some real evidence that could in some way link one of them to the crime."

When the Hardys reached their van, Frank found a slip of paper attached to the windshield. "Don't tell me it's a ticket," Joe said with a groan.

"Okay, I won't tell you," Frank said, stuffing the ticket in Joe's coat pocket.

"I think I've had enough of the big city for now," Joe said with a sigh. "What do you say we head back to nice, peaceful Bayport?"

"Fine with me," Frank said, unlocking the van.

The Hardys slept well that night. By eight-thirty the next morning, they were following a parade of cars over a suspension bridge that led back to the island of Manhattan. Across the bridge, hundreds of skyscrapers stood shoulder-to-shoulder against the clouds.

Joe parked the van in the same parking lot as the day before, but this time the Hardys planned to leave it there. "No tickets or traffic today," Joe said, shutting down the van engine. "From now on we travel the way most New Yorkers do."

The morning was cold, and the Hardys wasted no time finding stairs that led them down into the subway station and the underground network of trains that covered most of New York City.

It was rush hour, and the platform was packed with people on their way to work. Soon two headlights appeared, a rumbling was heard, then a glistening silver train rushed through a dark tunnel and slowed to a stop at the platform.

Doors slid open on each of the train's many cars, and people poured in and out of the car. When the doors closed, Frank and Joe were jammed together like sardines in a tin can. "Could you give me a little more room?" Joe asked Frank.

"Sure," Frank said. "I'll just tell the other ten thousand people to move over."

It was a relief to both Hardys when the doors finally opened at their stop uptown. Frank and Joe climbed a flight of steps and stood at the corner of Thirty-fourth Street and Sixth Avenue. The intersection was filled with people and cars, and across the street Frank spotted Macy's, the world's largest department store.

After walking a block and passing through a revolving door, the Hardys entered a lobby gleaming with polished black marble. This was the Empire State Building, but Frank and Joe were not there for sightseeing. The night before, they had learned from the telephone directory that this was where Fred Garfein's office was located.

The brothers rode a fast elevator to the seventy-ninth floor and entered a reception area. Frank told a secretary he and Joe wanted to speak with Garfein as part of a high school journalism project. The secretary spoke into an intercom box, a voice answered, then the secretary pointed at a door.

Beyond the door the Hardys found themselves in an office where vast windows showed a panoramic view of the city below. Fred Garfein was a middle-aged man with gray hair who looked tiny in comparison to the massive mahogany desk he sat behind.

"I don't understand what it is you kids want," Garfein said gruffly, "but since I'm a nice guy, I'll give you five minutes of my valuable time."

"We understand," Frank said, taking a seat across from Garfein, "that you've been trying to evict some of the tenants at four seventy-two

West Twenty-second Street. So you can renovate the apartments and charge higher rents."

"Everybody thinks us landlords are such villains," Garfein said. "But let me tell you what's not fair. The city's rent regulations."

"In what way?" Frank asked.

"The city says you can only raise the rent a small percent every time a tenant renews a lease," Garfein explained. "As a result, you've got all these old people who have been living in their apartments for twenty, thirty years, and they're paying rents way below the market value. That means the landlord loses money on those apartments."

"But—" Frank started.

"Wait until I'm finished," Garfein said, waving a hand. "In any other business a businessman has a right to charge whatever he wants. If a person is selling toys or gourmet food or dental floss, he can charge whatever the market will bear. That's the way this country is supposed to work. But the city won't let you do the same thing with apartments. And that, my friends, is not fair."

"The difference is—" Frank tried to say.

"And," Garfein continued, "if I'm forced to charge low rents on some of my apartments, that means I have to charge extra high rents on the other apartments in my fifteen buildings. So not only are these laws unfair to landlords, they're also unfair to the tenants who end up paying outrageously high rents."

"Except—" Frank said.

"And if I can't get people to pay those outrageously high rents," Garfein kept on, "that means I have to sell a building to cut my losses. But let me tell you something. That building on Twenty-second Street is prime real estate that I worked hard to buy, and I have no intention of selling it!"

Joe was standing at one of the windows, watching the conversation. Far below, people hurrying along the sidewalks appeared the size of insects. Joe figured that was probably just the way Fred Garfein viewed them.

"Does it bother you that elderly people, or artists, or people who have lost their jobs could lose their homes?" Joe asked Garfein.

"Stop, please, you're making me cry," Garfein said, swinging his feet onto his desk.

"Somehow I doubt that," Joe said.

"Look, I'm a businessman, not a saint," Garfein said. "If those people don't have a lot of money, maybe they should live in a cheaper neighborhood. And the old ones who haven't filed for an exemption should stay with their kids or go to an old folks home. It's not my problem."

"Well, I—" Joe began.

"And I'll tell you this," Garfein said, picking up a telephone receiver as if to dismiss the Hardys. "One way or another, I'm going to get those old geezers out. I guarantee it. All right, your five minutes are up. Get out of my office and have a nice day."

"Well, he's as charming as a shark," Joe said when the Hardys were back in the elevator.

"There's no question he's ruthless," Frank said. "But we still don't have any evidence . . ." His voice trailed off.

"What are you thinking?" Joe said.

"Remember how cold Karen Lee's building was?" Frank said. "Alex told us the temperature gauge was broken, but maybe Garfein instructed Alex to turn the heat off. Because he wants to freeze the older people out."

"Older people don't do well in the cold," Joe said. "A winter without heat could make at least some of them decide to move to a warmer building—or even a warmer climate."

"If we can prove the heat is turned off in that building," Frank said, "that would show how desperate Garfein is to get the tenants out— enough to use illegal tactics."

"That would be a real link," Joe said as the elevator opened at the lobby. "Evidence lending support to our theory that Garfein may have tried to do harm to Karen Lee. I agree with you that a big businessman like that would have hired someone for the job rather than do it himself."

Back in the wintry air, the brothers walked along Thirty-fourth Street. "Maybe Alex was the person Garfein hired," Frank said. "If Alex

59

would be willing to shut down the heat, maybe he would also be willing to kill Karen Lee. For a nice sum of money, of course. Which might be real attractive to a writer who has never been published."

"Except Alex doesn't seem to have much money now," Joe said, stopping on the sidewalk as the light turned red. "He's still the super."

"Maybe he didn't get paid because he bungled the attack," Frank suggested.

"I don't know," Joe said as the light changed to green. "In spite of his gory book titles, Alex doesn't seem like a killer to me."

"Neither does Nick Rodriguez," Frank said as they began to cross the street, "and you think he might be one."

"Good point," Joe said. "One thing I—"

"Look out!" Frank cried, grabbing Joe by the arm. A taxi was roaring full speed through a red light—straight for the Hardys.

# 7 Members of the Press

Frank jerked Joe out of the way, almost throwing him onto the sidewalk.

There was a screech of brakes and then a loud crunch of metal as the taxi hit the fender of another taxi making a turn. Both drivers stormed out of their cars and began to scream at each other in different languages. Immediately people gathered around to watch the shouting match, and a cop hurried over to break it up.

"There're a lot of dangerous things about this city," Joe commented as the Hardys gingerly crossed the street. "But you know, I think the taxi drivers might be the scariest."

The Hardys returned to the subway station, eager to catch a train back downtown so they could check in at the trial. Waiting on the crowded platform, Joe glanced down the tunnel. In the distance he could see repairmen working on the tracks, each one wearing a bright orange vest.

Soon a train came and rushed the Hardys downtown, where they emerged a few blocks from the courthouse. They walked along a street where some construction workers were busy tearing up the pavement to the earsplitting tune of a jackhammer.

"Hey, let me stop in here a second," Frank said, heading for the door of a small jewelry shop.

"Can I ask a stupid question?" Joe said, following Frank inside. "We've got two days left to solve this case. What are we doing here?"

A saleswoman stood behind a glass counter that displayed articles of gold and silver, some glittering with precious gems. Frank looked at a display area on top of the counter where the jewelry seemed more fun than expensive. "Callie is leaving town tomorrow to spend Christmas with her grandmother," Frank told Joe as he picked up a ring. "And I haven't gotten her a present yet."

"Say no more," Joe said. "If you mess up with a girlfriend's present, it's not a pretty sight."

Frank held one ring with a decorative flower and another with a decorative butterfly, both made from brightly painted enamel. "Those rings are very popular," the saleswoman told Frank. "Either one would be an excellent choice."

"Joe, what do you think?" Frank said, studying the two rings. "The flower or the butterfly?"

"I think the flower is better," Joe said, impatiently tapping his fingers on the counter.

"Uh . . . let's see," Frank said to the saleswoman. "I believe I'll take the butterfly."

"So much for my advice" Joe muttered.

"I'm sure the young woman will be very pleased," the saleswoman assured Frank with a courteous smile.

It was ten-thirty when the Hardys arrived at the criminal court building. The trial was taking a mid-morning break, and some of the spectators were stretching their legs in the gloomy corridor outside the courtroom. The Hardys caught Bernie Myers on his way back from the rest room and quickly explained what they had learned about Fred Garfein.

"Great, stay with it," Myers said, pulling some official papers from his rumpled suit. "And listen, I filed a motion this morning and got permission for you to view the physical evidence from the crime scene. Daggett put up a little fight, but the judge sided with me. Here, take these forms with you."

"Did you begin your defense?" Frank asked as he took the papers.

"I sure did," Myers said. "I'm starting with

character witnesses. People who can tell the jury what a decent and reliable person Nick is. I put Nick's parents on the stand this morning, and right after the break I'm putting Nellie on. The truth is, I expect her to be my best witness."

Suddenly the blond prosecutor, Patricia Daggett, was standing beside Myers, perfectly dressed and groomed again. Her high heels made her nearly as tall as Frank. "So these are your teenage PIs," Daggett said, her voice tinted with scorn.

"Yes, they are," Myers said proudly.

"Well, if they don't stop hounding Karen Lee," Daggett said, pointing a finger at Myers, "they may soon be keeping Nick Rodriguez company in jail."

Joe scowled at Daggett, but Frank was pleased to see the fashionable prosecutor was wearing a ring similar to the one he had just bought for Callie. Except, he noticed, Daggett had the flower instead of the butterfly. My taste must be okay, Frank thought.

"I'll have you know," Myers said, placing a hand on Joe's shoulder, "these teenagers are doing a terrific job. For example, they discovered that Karen Lee kept a set of keys to Nick Rodriguez's apartment, which disappeared right around the time of the crime. And that you knew about this yet failed to include it in your report to me."

64

"What's your point?" Daggett said.

"Some judges might consider that withholding evidence," Myers said. "A crime for which you could possibly be put in jail yourself."

"Bernie, I'll ignore that remark," Daggett said with a vicious smile. "I'll assume you're just in a bad mood because your case isn't going so well."

"What exactly does 'withholding evidence' mean?" Joe asked as Daggett stalked away.

"If the prosecution learns something important about a case," Myers explained, "the law says they have to share that information with the defense, no matter which side the information helps. And I've heard that Daggett has broken this law before."

Joe nodded, then moved toward the courtroom. Frank watched Daggett insert coins into a pay phone down the corridor. "How did she know we were the PIs working for you?" Frank asked Myers.

"When I filed the motion for you to look at the evidence," Myers said, "I had to explain who you were. You know, that you were teenagers and all that. Based on this, I guess she recognized you and also figured out you were the ones who spoke to Lee yesterday. That's one of the reasons Daggett is so good. She makes it her business to know absolutely everything that concerns her job."

"And I suppose she really wants to win this

case because Karen Lee worked in the prosecutor's office for a short while," Frank remarked.

"No, Pat Daggett always wants to win," Myers said, scoffing. "You see, all the prosecutors are classified as assistant district attorneys. And they have to answer to the head district attorney, which is one of the most powerful positions in the city. Well, when the current district attorney retires, Daggett hopes to be in line for the job."

"So ambition, not justice, is what makes her want to win so badly," Frank said, understanding.

"Exactly," Myers said, adjusting his tie. "I'd better get back in there now. I'll see you around later, or give me a call at my office tonight."

"Good luck," Frank called as Myers entered the courtroom.

As Myers walked away, Joe returned. "I was looking for that Velloni woman, but I didn't see her," Joe told Frank. "I think some of those guys over there are also reporters, though. Maybe they can give us some information on her."

Nearby, a half dozen men were clustered together in conversation. After a moment of eavesdropping, the Hardys learned they were all members of the press.

Leaning against the wall, not talking to the others, was the clean-cut young man Joe had seen the day before across the street from Karen Lee's

66

apartment building. Because he looked nicer than the other reporters, Joe approached him first. "Do you by any chance know Lisa Velloni?" Joe asked.

The young man shook his head, then looked down.

"He seems awfully shy for a journalist," Joe said, returning to Frank.

"Excuse us," Frank said, approaching the other men. "Do any of you know Lisa Velloni?"

Chuckles came from the group, making it clear these men found Velloni an object of fun. A short man with a toothpick dangling from his lips spoke first. "Oh, sure, we all know Lunatic Lisa. Why?"

"Just looking for a little information on her," Frank said as if he were a fellow reporter.

A man with a long ponytail spoke next. "Most of us work for various tabloids, but Velloni's on her own. A freelancer. She just gets a story and then tries to sell it to whoever will buy."

A man who hadn't shaven in several days added, "No one wants to hire her on a regular basis. Even the tabloid publishers think she's too bananas."

Again, the men all chuckled.

"Until recently she had only done real small-time stuff," the short reporter informed the Hardys. "You know, tidbits about minor TV stars and people with strange pets. Things like that."

"What happened recently?" Joe asked.

"When Karen Lee first landed her role on *Days of Destiny*," the man with the ponytail explained, "Velloni did a story on her. A 'struggling actress gets her first big break in television' type of thing. Then when this attempted murder story broke, Velloni got exclusive rights to Lee because they were already acquainted."

"So now she's the only one who gets interviews with Lee," the short one said. "Which means she's getting paid some decent money for her stories."

"More than any of us," another man muttered.

"And she's even been approached about doing a book on Karen Lee," another man grumbled.

"Which could make her some really good dough," another man said bitterly.

"Does Lisa Velloni ever do anything illegal to get her stories?" Joe asked. The question was immediately followed by a round of snickering.

"What's so funny?" Frank asked.

"Lisa will do anything to get a story," the unshaven man said. "And I mean *anything*."

"There's a rumor she once sent a bunch of threatening letters to a famous actor," the short one said, gesturing with his toothpick. "Under a fake name, of course. It was a stunt, you see, just so she could have an intriguing story to report. No one knows if it's true or not, but I'm—"

68

Before he could finish, a pair of hands shot out, and the short reporter went flying backward into the wall. As others stepped back in surprise, Joe whipped around to see Lisa Velloni glaring at the short man as if she planned to kill him.

# 8 Cross-examination

"What's the big idea, Lisa?" the short man shouted. "Shoving me against the wall like that!"

"You were telling lies about me!" Velloni shouted back. "I've told you a hundred times, short boy, I never sent those letters!"

Like the day before, Velloni was wearing a turtleneck sweater and a leather miniskirt. Her eyes were on fire, and she was now moving toward the short reporter with her fist ready to deliver a good punch in the face.

"Hey, hey, hey, take it easy," Frank said, pulling Velloni back by the shoulders.

"Let them slug it out," the unshaven man said. "We can all place bets." The other press members clapped and laughed uproariously.

"Listen, you creeps," Velloni said as Frank held on to her. "I'm a respectable reporter. More respectable than any of you. Though that certainly isn't saying very much!"

"What about the time you jumped in front of a police car and then made them take you along for a high-speed chase?" one of the men called out.

"You guys are just jealous because I got exclusive rights to Karen Lee," Velloni said. "You think journalism is a man's job and women are only qualified for the powder puff stories. And you boys just hate when a woman gets the better of you!"

"Ooh, Lisa, we get so scared when you talk that way," one of the men said.

"You guys have been making fun of me for years," Velloni said, shaking her fist in the air, "but not anymore. Just you wait."

Before things could go any farther, a bailiff announced the trial was about to resume, and the reporters all scurried like mice back to the courtroom.

"Miss Velloni," Frank said as he released her, "could we talk to you a second?"

"What about?" Velloni said, eyeing Frank and Joe suspiciously. "Aren't you the guys who gave me grief yesterday?" Frank wondered if she also recognized them from last night on the rooftop.

71

"My brother and I stumbled on some information related to the Karen Lee case," Joe said, "and we thought you might like to know about it." Joe figured this was the best way to get Velloni to speak with them.

"Right now I've got to get back to the trial," Velloni said, interest sparkling in her eyes. "Can I meet you later? Right here, quarter after five?"

"Sure," Joe said.

"Perfect," Velloni said, rushing away.

The Hardys took a seat in the back row of the courtroom, figuring they would watch some of the trial before continuing their investigation. First Bernie Myers called Nellie to the witness stand.

Myers got Nellie to explain that Nick had always been a model boy when they were growing up, never once getting into trouble with the law. She also explained that Nick was a very loving person, someone she and her parents could always count on.

Joe noticed a middle-aged couple sitting in the front row. By the family resemblance, he could tell they were Nick and Nellie's parents.

"Myers was right," Frank whispered to Joe. "Nellie seems to be making an excellent impression on the spectators and jury."

When Myers finished with his questioning, he sat down and gave Nick's arm a supportive squeeze. Frank watched Patricia Daggett stand for the cross-examination. She studied Nellie a moment, and Nellie looked right back at her, not the least bit intimidated by the prosecutor.

"Miss Rodriguez," Daggett said pleasantly, "I take it you and your twin brother are very close."

"Yes, we are," Nellie said.

"And I take it you've looked after each other a good deal over the years," Daggett said.

"Yes, of course we have," Nellie said.

"In fact," Daggett said with a smile, "I'll bet when you were kids, if one of you did something wrong, the other would help cover it up."

"Objection," Myers called out to the judge. "Miss Daggett has no way of knowing this."

"Sustained," the judge said with a nod, indicating that he agreed with Myers. "Stick to the line of questioning," he said sternly to Daggett.

"Let me put that a different way," Daggett said to Nellie. "*Did* you help cover for each other when one of you did something wrong?"

"Objection," Myers called to the judge. "This question has no bearing on the case."

"On the contrary," Daggett told the judge, "this is a very important point."

"Overruled, Mr. Myers," the judge said. "You may proceed," he said to Nellie.

Daggett returned her gaze to Nellie, waiting for an answer. "Yes," Nellie said calmly. "I suppose Nick and I helped cover for each other when we were kids. But that doesn't mean—"

"And now that you two are adults," Daggett said, walking slowly toward the jury box, "I suppose you would still do just about anything to help your brother. Is that correct?"

"Within reason, I suppose," Nellie said.

"In fact," Daggett said, resting a hand on the railing as she gazed at the jury, "I suppose you might *pretend* your brother did not try to kill his ex-fiancée when, in fact, you know that he did."

A flurry of whispers blew through the courtroom. "Objection!" Myers cried out, rising to his feet. "Your Honor, the prosecutor is way out of bounds here! She has no way of knowing if—"

"Sustained," the judge said, casting a stern look at Daggett. "I will ask the jury to ignore that last comment by the prosecutor."

"He can ask the jury to ignore the comment," Joe whispered to Frank, "but they still heard it."

"Which is exactly what Daggett wanted," Frank whispered back. "She sure is sneaky."

Daggett now approached Nellie, her high heels clicking on the courtroom floor. Something about the way she moved reminded Frank of a spider spinning a web. "Miss Rodriguez," Daggett said, "is it true that approximately one

74

month before the crime you and your brother attended a Fourth of July party?"

"That is correct," Nellie said, a worried look crossing her face.

Myers glanced at Nick, obviously unsure of what was coming. Nick kept his eyes on his sister, but Joe could see Nick's fist was clenched.

"And I believe," Daggett said to Nellie, "Karen Lee was also at this party, wasn't she?"

"Yes, she was," Nellie said quietly.

Frank noticed Karen Lee sitting nearby. She was nervously fingering her silky hair.

"Tell me," Daggett said, standing near Nellie. "At this party, did you happen to witness an argument between your brother and Miss Lee?"

"Objection," Myers said. "This has no—"

"Overruled," the judge cut in. "Miss Rodriguez, answer the question, please."

"Yes," Nellie said. "I witnessed an argument between my brother and Miss Lee at this party."

"What was this argument about?" Daggett asked.

"Karen had broken off her engagement to my brother a month before this party, and he was still upset about it," Nellie explained, shifting in her chair.

"I understand there were some real fireworks that night," Daggett said with a sly smile. "And I don't mean in the sky. Tell me, did your brother become angry during this argument?"

"People often get angry during arguments," Nellie said, struggling to stay composed.

"Just answer the question, please," Daggett insisted.

"Yes, he became angry," Nellie admitted.

"Did he yell at Miss Lee?" Daggett asked.

"Yes, he raised his voice a bit," Nellie said. Joe could see that she was growing irritated with the prosecutor.

"And did he make an especially threatening comment to Miss Lee?" Daggett asked, fixing her cold eyes on Nellie. "A comment that was over-heard by a number of the people present?"

"Yes," Nellie snapped, "but it was merely a figure of speech. He didn't mean—"

"What was that comment?" Daggett said firmly.

Nellie hesitated—as if she was afraid to an-swer, Frank thought.

"I will remind you," Daggett told Nellie, "that you have sworn to tell the whole truth up here. Failure to do so would be a criminal act."

Nellie took a deep breath, then answered the question. "My brother said, 'Karen, sometimes you make me so mad I want to kill you.'"

Cries and whispers resounded throughout the room. As the judge banged his gavel for order, Frank glanced at the jury box. Just about every member of the jury was staring harshly at Nick Rodriguez.

"No further questions," Daggett said, returning to her table with a satisfied expression.

"Yeah, Daggett's good," Frank said after a sigh. "So much for Nellie's excellent impression."

Knowing they had better get back to work, the Hardys left the courthouse and walked to a small park across the street. The day had warmed a bit, but a gray pall darkened the sky, as if reflecting the trial's grim turn of events.

"I doubt Nick really meant what he said at that party," Joe said as he and Frank sat on a bench, "but Daggett sure made it seem as if he did. And it doesn't help that this information came from the mouth of Nick's own twin sister."

"At this point," Frank said, "it may not be enough for us to come up with evidence suggesting someone else *might* have done the crime. After what just happened, to get Nick off, I think we need to *prove* someone else did it. And soon."

Joe looked around, considering this statement. There were other courthouses in the area. Big, impressive buildings where people came to argue every imaginable legal matter—crimes, lawsuits, divorces, child custody, even traffic tickets.

Suddenly a flock of pigeons fluttered away. Looking up, Joe noticed a young man in a worn leather jacket standing near the bench. He had a smirk on his face and a very bizarre hairdo. Half his hair was dyed bright red, the other half bright green.

"Mind if I sit down?" the man asked.

"Not at all," Joe said, scooting over to make room at the end of the bench.

But instead of sitting at the end, the man squeezed in between Joe and Frank.

"Dude," Joe said, annoyed, "we're having a private conversation here."

Very calmly, the man pulled out a knife from his pocket. He pushed a button, and a long blade shot out.

"Is that right?" the man said, touching the blade to Joe's throat. "Well, right now, I want you to have a little conversation with me."

# 9 A Shred of Evidence

Frank thought about grabbing the knife, but the man turned to him, keeping the blade on Joe. "You make a move for me," the man warned, "and your brother gets cut. Got it?"

Frank nodded in response. "So, what is it you want to discuss?" he said as calmly as he could.

"A very simple business matter," the man said. "I've been instructed by a certain party to tell you two to stop being so nosy. If you don't, I might have to cut both your noses off. Then you won't smell so good. Get it?"

The man with the red-and-green hair laughed a maniacal laugh. Then, as if nothing unusual had happened, he returned the knife to his jacket pocket and walked away.

Joe sprang to his feet, ready to follow the man, but Frank held him back.

"What are you doing?" Joe said, his blue eyes flashing with anger. "He pulled a knife on me! Let's go get the jerk!"

"That's precisely why we're *not* going to go get the jerk," Frank said, holding Joe tightly. "Violence isn't going to get us anywhere. But I think this helps us prove Nick's innocence. Obviously the real culprit told this guy to scare us off the case."

"Not necessarily," Joe said as he watched the red-green man disappear around the corner of a nearby building. "Maybe Garfein sent him, not because he tried to have Karen Lee killed but just because he doesn't like us nosing into his affairs."

"Maybe, but I doubt it," Frank said, finally releasing Joe. "Come on. Since I didn't let you flatten that creep, I'll buy you lunch."

Soon the Hardys were seated in a delicatessen that was noisy with conversation and clattering plates. Joe was devouring a sandwich piled high with pastrami, while Frank was working on a sandwich of turkey and Swiss cheese.

"Okay," Joe said, chewing away. "Even though I think Nick is guilty, I've come up with another theory. It's far-fetched, but it makes some sense."

"Let's hear it," Frank said.

"Those reporters said Lisa Velloni will do anything to get a story," Joe said. "They hinted she might even do something illegal."

"She also seemed eager to prove a woman can get a good story as well as a man," Frank added.

"When Lee first got her soap role last May, Velloni did a story on her," Joe said, lifting a bottle of root beer. "Now, maybe, just maybe, Velloni staged a murder attempt on Lee. She probably didn't intend to kill her. But she knew it would make a story as juicy as this pastrami. And she figured she could get exclusive rights to the story because she and Lee were already acquainted."

"I don't know, Joe—" Frank started.

"Remember," Joe continued, "getting exclusive rights to Lee is a big break for Velloni. This trial isn't a powder-puff piece, and Velloni has the inside track on it. She's making more money than the other reporters, and when the trial's over she could even get a book deal. And you've seen yourself how angry and aggressive she is."

"Okay, I can see how that might be possible," Frank said after a bite of his sandwich. "But then why would she frame Nick Rodriguez?"

"To keep suspicion away from herself," Joe said, picking up a big pickle. "Or perhaps to make for an even juicier story."

"But could she be so determined that she'd let an innocent man go to prison?" Frank asked.

"I don't think we can answer that until we get to know her better," Joe said, chomping on the pickle. "And remember, it probably was her we saw in Nick's apartment last night. And if she has access to Nick's apartment, she could have been the one who planted the evidence under the mattress."

"All right," Frank said. "We'll put her on the suspect list. We'll have a chance to feel her out when we meet her later this afternoon."

"So we've now got three suspects to pursue," Joe said. "Fred Garfein, John Q., and Lisa Velloni."

"But we still need evidence linking at least one of them to the crime," Frank said, wiping his mouth with a napkin. "And what we really need is proof that one of them did it."

"And we need it by tomorrow," Joe said, sliding his empty plate away. "Good luck to us."

After lunch, the Hardys split up. They agreed to call the telephone answering machine at their home in one hour, in case they had any messages to tell each other. Joe set off to locate the apartment of John Q., and Frank walked a few blocks to police headquarters for a look at whatever physical evidence had been collected from the crime scene.

On the eleventh floor, Frank was taken into a

82

room containing aisle after aisle of floor-to-ceiling shelves. The shelves housed cardboard boxes, each labeled with a number. This was where the police stored evidence collected from every crime scene in Manhattan. They kept the evidence on hand until the crime was completely solved.

Frank followed Sergeant Tyrell, a burly policeman with a bushy mustache, down a long aisle. "Frank Hardy, huh?" Tyrell said. "You aren't related to Fenton Hardy, are you?"

"He's my father," Frank said with pride.

"No kidding," Tyrell said, glancing back at Frank. "I got to know him a bit when I first joined the force. Terrific fellow. He helped me out of a few jams."

Frank and Joe's father, Fenton, had worked a number of years for the New York City Police Department before he became a renowned private investigator.

Sergeant Tyrell stopped and pulled down a cardboard box, which he set on the floor. "It says here," Tyrell said, studying a file of papers he had brought, "the gloves and ski mask are being kept at the courthouse because the prosecutor is using them in the trial. The coat and knife have not been found."

"So what's in the box?" Frank asked.

"Not much," Tyrell said, still looking at the file. "It says these are items the police collected from the floor right near where the crime took place. Karen Lee claims she swept her floor shortly before the attack, and the police collected these items shortly after the attack."

"In other words," Frank said, "there's a chance these items came from the attacker."

"It's possible," Tyrell said as he opened the box and reached inside. "Let's have a look."

Tyrell handed Frank a sealed plastic packet. The only thing inside was a tiny pink item. It was oval and no bigger than a fingernail fragment. "This is a small piece of metal with painted enamel on it," Tyrell said, checking the file. "No one has any idea what it is, and it may not have anything at all to do with the crime."

Frank stared at the piece of pink enamel a few moments, trying to imagine what it might be. Nothing came to mind. "Anything else?" he said, handing the packet back to Sergeant Tyrell.

"Just this," Tyrell said, handing Frank another sealed plastic packet. This one contained a few tiny shreds of a yarnlike substance in a color somewhere between gray and beige.

"These are carpet or rug fibers," Tyrell explained. "They don't match with any carpets or rugs found in the apartment or place of work of Lee or Rodriguez, but they still could have come off one of those two people."

Frank was thinking about how the fibers might be of use. "Let's say I had a suspect for this crime," Frank said, "and I found this person had a carpet or rug that matched these fibers exactly. Would that help point a finger at that person?"

"It certainly could," Tyrell said. "*If* you could match those fibers exactly."

"How would I do that?" Frank asked.

"First you would have to gather some samples from that person's home or office," Tyrell explained. "Then you would need an expert to compare them with these samples. We have a crime lab where specialists are trained for that type of work, but you wouldn't be allowed access to it."

"Not even if it would help establish the truth?" Frank said with a hopeful look.

"Our facilities are for the police and prosecutors only," Tyrell said with a shrug. "You're lucky the judge is even letting you look at this stuff."

"But if, say, *you* wanted to send something to the crime lab for analysis," Frank said, "you could do it. Because you're a policeman. Right?"

"That's not really my job," Tyrell said, scratching his mustache. "But I know some of those people fairly well, and, yes, I probably could. But that doesn't mean I could do it for someone else who's *not* a cop or prosecutor."

"Not even if that person was the son of Fenton Hardy," Frank said, locking eyes with Tyrell. Frank did not like to throw his father's name around, but sometimes it proved helpful. Most folks who knew Fenton Hardy liked and admired him a great deal.

Tyrell scratched his mustache some more, all the while looking at Frank. "Okay, kid," he said, lowering his voice. "If you get some fibers, I'll send them and these over to the crime lab and have them run a quick check. But you need to keep real quiet about it. Understand?"

"Quiet is my middle name," Frank said, handing the plastic packet with the fibers back to Tyrell.

Joe climbed out of a subway station and walked east. Right away, Joe could see that this area, the East Village, was where the hip people hung out. Most of the people passing by looked to be about his age, Joe thought. Most were dressed in funky clothing, and many of them had their hair dyed wild colors, from orange to aqua.

Joe walked along a block lined with stores that sold things like old rock' n' roll records and super-cool sunglasses.

Stopping at a pay phone, Joe dialed his home number, then punched in the code to retrieve any messages. There was a message from Frank, who explained that if Joe got into John Q.'s apartment and if there was a carpet or rug there, Joe should collect a few fibers from it. He then said Joe should meet him near Karen Lee's apartment house in one hour.

Soon Joe was walking along a block lined with run-down apartment buildings, most of them with graffiti scrawled on their walls. Joe approached the front door of the building with the address that matched the one from John Q.'s letter. Joe buzzed 4F, John's apartment. There was no answer.

Joe waited a moment while a girl with a ring in her nose passed by. I must be the squarest guy in the neighborhood, Joe thought as he pulled a metal strip from his pocket. Every now and then, the Hardys found it necessary to pick a lock, and this was one of those times, Joe figured. After a little fiddling, Joe managed to get the door open.

The hallway was dimly lit, and the walls were in need of a paint job. Joe climbed several sets of steps and came finally to the door of apartment 4F.

Joe knocked. After getting no answer, he picked the lock on the door. Then he stepped into the apartment's living room and relocked the door.

Joe thought the place was surprisingly neat and well decorated. Posters of movies and plays hung on the walls, and some top-of-the-line audio and video equipment rested on the shelves of an entertainment center.

Joe heard a click. He froze and listened. Was someone in the apartment? There seemed to be another room or two he had not yet checked. Then Joe was aware of a low, whirring sound.

After a look at the entertainment center, Joe realized the VCR had just switched on. John Q. must have preset it to tape a program, Joe figured. Wondering what the program was, Joe pushed a button on the cable box, and the television lit up.

Suddenly Joe was face-to-face with Karen Lee.

She was on TV, wearing a nurse's uniform and telling a worried-looking woman that her little son was going to be all right. Joe realized John had preset the recorder to videotape the day's episode of Lee's soap opera, *Days of Destiny.*

Joe watched the show briefly. At this moment, he realized, Karen Lee was coming into millions of homes all over the country. The scary part was, she had no control over who got to know her and develop feelings for her. If a crazy person wanted to watch her every day, that person was free to do so.

After turning off the TV, Joe noticed the floor was covered with a gray carpet. He pulled a few fibers and put them inside his wallet.

Joe heard another click. He thought some other gadget must have switched on or off, but he could not figure out what it was. Then he realized the sound had come from the front door. It was the sound of a key turning in a lock.

Someone was about to enter the apartment.

# 10 The Face on
## the Screen

All Joe had time to do was duck behind a sofa.

Crouched in hiding, Joe heard the door open. Then he heard shoes moving across the gray carpet.

A moment later, there was a click, and the television came on. It was *Days of Destiny* again, and Joe heard Karen Lee discussing some medical situation with a doctor.

Joe stole a peek around the side of the sofa. He was shocked by whom he saw. It was the clean-cut young man Joe had *thought* was a reporter. He was standing right in front of the TV, the light from the screen reflecting in his wire-rimmed glasses.

Joe realized this was John Q. He was at the trial not as a reporter but because he wanted to watch Karen Lee in person. That's also why he was standing across the street from her apartment building. Joe had just assumed he was a reporter.

"Hi," the young man spoke. "How are you?"

At first Joe thought John Q. might be talking to him, but he was still facing the screen. Then Joe realized John Q. was talking to Karen Lee on TV as if she were actually in the room.

"Oh, I'm not too bad," John Q. told the screen version of Lee. "Sorry I had to leave the trial today, but they needed me to come in to work at the video store a little early. You looked awfully beautiful in there. It's all I can do to stop myself from going up and talking to you. But maybe I will someday. Who knows? Since things didn't work out with Nick, maybe they'll work out with me."

Maybe he's the one, Joe thought. He was seeing that John Q. might indeed be crazy enough to have staged the murder attempt on Karen Lee. He felt a sudden thrill, the kind he usually got when closing in on a criminal.

Then John Q. took off his ski vest and walked into another room. Joe briefly considered sticking around to watch more, but he decided he'd better take the opportunity to slip out the door.

Thirty minutes later, Joe arrived in Chelsea, on the corner of the block where Karen Lee lived.

Sleet was now slanting down from the sky, and Joe found Frank under the canvas awning of a small food market.

"You were right," Frank said after Joe had explained about his East Village discovery. "John Q. sounds like a nut."

"And here are the carpet fibers from his place," Joe said, pulling them from his wallet.

"Let's see," Frank said, putting the fibers in one of several plastic packets he had been given by Sergeant Tyrell. "They look like they could be the right color. Thanks, Joe."

"So we know John Q. is seriously obsessed with Lee," Joe said, zipping his coat up higher. "Which lends support to my theory that he may have staged the attack on her in order to frame Rodriguez."

"True," Frank said, watching people hurry by to get out of the icy sleet. "But it's still a shaky theory. We still need some kind of hard evidence linking John to the crime."

"But the carpet fibers could do it," Joe said.

"If we're lucky," Frank said. "Right now, let's move on to the Garfein-Alex theory. That's why I wanted to meet here. You'll go to Alex's apartment. If he's there, talk to him, especially about his relationship with Garfein. If he's not there, get in and have a look around. Either way, if there's a carpet or rug, pick some fibers."

91

"And while I'm in another potentially dangerous situation," Joe said, "where will you be? Doing some late Christmas shopping?"

"I'll be in the basement," Frank told Joe. "Checking to see if the heat has been turned off. And we all know how dangerous basements can be."

Frank and Joe hurried down the block, bracing themselves against the freezing pellets of sleet. "Before we visit Alex's place," Joe suggested, "how about we take another look in Lee's apartment? I saw a bunch of fan letters in there, and now I'm thinking there may be more of them from John Q. Maybe one that contains a link to the crime."

"Even if it does," Frank pointed out, "the letter wouldn't be allowed in court because we got it by being there illegally. Remember, we're not really supposed to do that."

"Okay, but if we find a letter from John," Joe argued, "maybe we can have Myers gain legal access to it. He can tell the judge it's important that he sees all of Karen Lee's fan letters. That could work."

"You're starting to think like a lawyer," Frank said as the Hardys came to Lee's building.

The Hardys made their way past the building's front door and climbed the stairs to the third floor. Stepping out of the stairwell, Frank noticed the door with a small window that Nick had spoken of. Did Nick really see a face through that window? Frank believed he had. But whose face was it?

Joe picked the lock to 3C, and the Hardys entered Lee's apartment. "Still no heat," Frank said, finding the place even colder than before.

At the desk, Joe found the manila envelope filled with fan letters that he had seen the day before. "None of them is opened," Joe said, thumbing quickly through the letters.

"Any of them from John Q.?" Frank asked.

"Nope," Joe replied.

A bell jingled, causing Joe to jump. Then Joe realized it was Karen Lee's telephone.

An answering machine turned on. "Hi, I can't get to the phone right now," a recorded message with Lee's voice said. "Please leave a message."

Frank and Joe both turned to the machine.

"Hello, Karen," a male voice said on the machine. "My name is Zeke Washington. I've sent you several letters in the past few months, but I haven't heard from you yet. Listen, Karen, in the name of justice, it's urgent I talk to you about the issue I discussed in my letters. It's a little complicated getting hold of me, but I left the information on how to do this in all three of my letters. Please, please contact me. Goodbye."

Then the man hung up.

"He said it's urgent he talk to her in the name of justice," Frank said thoughtfully. "Do you think this has something to do with the case?"

"I don't know," Joe said, leafing through the

fan letters again. "But I do see some letters from a Zeke Washington."

Joe showed Frank one of the letters. In the upper lefthand corner of the envelope, the following return address was written:

Zeke Washington, Inmate 82658
Ossining Correctional Facility
Ossining, NY 10562-5498

"This address is for a state prison about fifty miles north of here," Frank said. "Sing Sing. Zeke Washington is a prisoner there. What do you suppose he wants?"

"Why don't we open his letters?" Joe said.

Frank ran a finger over the envelope. "It's tempting," he said, "but I think we should resist. Even if we sealed them back up, Lee might notice. Opening someone's mail—at least, if it's not in the trash—is a federal offense."

"Then maybe we could try and contact Zeke ourselves," Joe suggested.

"Maybe," Frank said, setting down the letter.

After returning the letters to the manila envelope, the Hardys went back to the first floor. From there Frank took a flight of steps down to the basement, and Joe stepped outside onto the stoop.

There was an intercom box in front of the building with buttons corresponding to every tenant's name and apartment number. Joe buzzed 1B. Alex's apartment. No point in letting

Alex know he had already been inside the building, Joe figured.

"Who is it?" a voice spoke through the box.

"It's Joe Hardy," Joe called. "I was in the neighborhood and figured I'd stop by. I'd like to hear a little more about your mystery novels. If you're not too busy, that is."

There was a buzz on the electrical lock, and Joe pushed the front door open. Alex was standing in his doorway on the first floor, wearing jeans and a pullover sweater. "I was just doing some writing," Alex said with a friendly smile. "But I guess I could spare a fellow writer a few minutes."

Joe followed Alex into the apartment, which he noticed was also quite cold. It was only one room with a small kitchen off to the side. Most of the furnishings were of the flea market variety, including a couch that was actually an abandoned car seat. Joe noticed a tattered, multicolored Persian rug on the floor.

Alex sat by a table with a computer. "My place isn't too impressive," Alex said. "Struggling writers aren't the richest people."

Yes, he sure looks as if he could use some extra cash, Joe thought. But how far would he go to get it? Would he try to kill someone?

"You know what you should do," Joe said, taking a seat on the car seat couch. "Base a story on the murder attempt in this building."

"Great minds think alike," Alex said. "I'm planning on it. I'll probably change a few details, though, to make the story more terrifying."

"It's pretty terrifying already," Joe said.

Alex leaned forward, fixing his falcon eyes on Joe. "Books tend to sell better if there's an actual murder," he almost whispered. "So in my story the victim will really be killed."

There was something strange about the way Alex had said this. Joe got the impression Alex might be talking about something more real than a book. In a funny sort of way, Joe thought, maybe Alex was saying he was the one who tried to murder Karen Lee. Maybe he was also hinting that he would try it again—and get it right on the second attempt.

"Do you know who the murderer will be?" Joe asked, meeting Alex's gaze.

"I have a good idea," Alex replied.

"Who is it?" Joe asked.

A mysterious smile played across Alex's lips, then he said, "You'll have to read the book."

"The day it comes out," Joe said quietly.

Then Alex looked away from Joe, as if he had just thought of something. He stared out the window, watching the sleet tap against the pane.

Joe noticed a shoebox on the floor that contained a collection of labeled keys. Joe figured they were keys to all the apartments in the building.

"How long have you been super here?" Joe asked.

"About ten years," Alex said, still looking off. What is he thinking? Joe wondered.

"How's the landlord?" Joe asked. "I mean, you know, is he a nice guy to work for?"

"Uh, Joe, would you excuse me a second?" Alex said, suddenly picking an envelope up off the table. "I got a piece of 1C's mail by mistake, and I want to slip it under his door."

"Go on," Joe said. "I won't steal anything."

The moment Alex left the apartment, Joe knelt by the Persian rug and began plucking out carpet fibers, making sure to get a sample of each color that was close to beige or gray.

Meanwhile Frank was moving through a darkened storage room in the basement. A dampness crept through the concrete floor and walls, making the room even chillier than the apartments. Using a pen-sized flashlight, Frank saw pieces of lumber, power tools, paint cans, a snow shovel, mops, brooms, and other building maintenance supplies.

At the far end of the room, he came to a door that was painted scarlet. With a rusty creak, the door opened, and Frank entered.

The concrete room was bare except for a metal contraption about the size of a compact car. Frank knew this was the boiler. Numerous pipes fed into the boiler, and a small flame danced underneath it.

Frank played his flashlight over the boiler, searching for the heat control. If the heat was turned off, Frank would know Garfein and Alex were using illegal tactics to get rid of tenants. And if they were willing to turn off the heat in winter, they might be willing to commit murder.

Then Frank heard footsteps in the storage room. He quickly flipped off his flashlight and hid behind the boiler. Soon he heard what sounded like something being picked up off a shelf, and then the footsteps walked closer.

With a creak, the door to the boiler room opened. Frank waited. He heard only silence.

Frank peered around the edge of the boiler. The flames shed just enough light for Frank to make out the shadowy shape of a person.

"Is there someone in here?" a low voice said.

Frank now recognized the person as Alex. And he realized Alex was holding a very large ax.

# 11 Danger in the Basement

Keeping his foot in the doorway, Alex flipped a switch. A single light bulb illuminated the room.

"If you're in here," Alex said, gripping the ax with both hands, "you'd better tell me now."

Frank realized it would be only seconds before Alex found him. "It's me," Frank said, stepping out from hiding, his hands in the air.

"This is a funny place to be working on a high school journalism assignment," Alex commented.

By the light of the boiler flames, Frank could see Alex's piercing eyes. He decided to tell the truth. "My brother and I suspected Fred Garfein may have ordered you to turn off the heat. As a tactic for driving away the building's elderly tenants. I came here to check the heat control."

Alex let the boiler room door close. "When Garfein told me you guys had visited him," he said, "I figured something was up. Then when I was talking with Joe in my apartment, I realized you might be somewhere in the building. I have to tell you, Frank, I don't like prowlers in my basement. I had a few things stolen last month."

"Sorry," Frank said. "I shouldn't be here."

"I don't like liars, either," Alex said, moving slowly toward Frank. "You see, I get the feeling you're still not telling me the complete truth."

"What am I leaving out?" Frank said, keeping both eyes on the ax.

A creepy smile crossed Alex's lips. "Maybe you also suspect Garfein had something to do with the murder attempt on Karen Lee," he said. "Maybe you also think he paid someone to do it. And maybe you even suspect I'm the one he hired."

"You're very perceptive," Frank said.

"You have to be pretty devious if you're going to surprise a guy who writes murder mysteries," Alex said, fixing his intense eyes on Frank.

With a creak, the door opened.

"Then I guess I'm pretty devious," Joe said, standing in the doorway, holding an iron crowbar.

100

Alex was startled, Frank relieved.

"When you didn't come back right away," Joe continued, "I realized you might be looking for Frank. I know blood is your favorite color, Alex, but why don't you put down that ax?"

Alex was now between the two Hardys. "Why don't you put down that crowbar?" Alex told Joe.

"Deal," Joe told Alex. At the same time, Joe and Alex put their weapons on the ground.

"Now," Alex said, holding up his hands, "why don't we try swapping the truth? Because I think we've got some serious misunderstandings here."

"Deal," Frank said. "You go first."

"Okay," Alex said, shoving up the sleeves of his sweater. "Mr. Garfein isn't crazy about Karen Lee because she's messing up his renovation plans. But neither he nor I had anything to do with the murder attempt. As far as the heat goes . . ."

Alex opened the door of a small metal box mounted on the wall. Aiming his flashlight beam at it, Frank saw a switch between the words On and Off. The switch was obviously turned on.

"This is the heat control," Alex explained. "You can plainly see the switch is in the on position. Even though the boiler flames are going, the heat isn't working because the temperature gauge on the boiler needs to be replaced. I've been trying to get the repairmen to come,

101

but they keep canceling on me. Hopefully they'll be here this afternoon. That's my truth. Now it's your turn."

In the name of fair play, the Hardys told Alex they were detectives working for the defense of Nick Rodriguez. They revealed everything, except for the fact that they had just broken into Lee's apartment.

Alex listened, fascinated. When the tale was done, he said, "So you guys are detectives, huh?"

"Yes, we are," Joe answered.

"Have you worked on many cases?" Alex asked.

"Plenty," Frank said.

"What type?" Alex asked.

"All types," Joe said. "Theft, attempted murder, sabotage, kidnapping, dognapping, catnapping."

"How old are you?" Alex said.

"I'm eighteen, he's seventeen," Frank replied.

"Wow!" Alex cried, lighting up with excitement. "You know what I should do? I should write a book about you guys. A real-life profile of the Hardy brothers, teenage detectives. A book like that could really take off. And I'm talking best-seller here. I could make you guys famous!"

Alex looked from Frank to Joe, as if expecting them to be thrilled with his idea.

"Do we want to be famous, Frank?" Joe asked.

"I don't think so," Frank said, matter-of-factly. "We get into enough trouble as it is."

Alex looked crushed. "All right, listen," he said, not letting go of the idea. "Take some time to think this over. Really think about it. If you change your mind, you know where to find me."

"In the basement with an ax," Frank remarked with a grin. "Really, Alex, you should get out more."

When the Hardys left the building, daylight was fading and the sleet had stopped, leaving the streets and sidewalks wet. "Well, what do you think—do Garfein and Alex stay on the suspect list?" Joe asked Frank.

"I guess so," Frank said, zipping up his coat, "but without the heat angle, there's still no evidence linking either one of them to the crime."

"I got some fibers from a rug in Alex's apartment," Joe said. "Maybe those will match up."

"We can only hope," Frank said, checking his watch. "Come on, we'd better put on some speed. We're supposed to meet Velloni at a quarter past five."

On the way to the subway, Frank called Sing Sing prison from a pay phone. He discovered they did have a prisoner named Zeke Washington there. He also learned the next day was a visiting day. The Hardys could meet Washington then.

It was almost dark by the time the Hardys reached the criminal court building. Rushing up the concrete steps, they ran into Nellie and Myers, who were leaving for dinner, then for a visit with Nick. They both looked exhausted from the day's trial. Frank and Joe quickly ran through the events of their day.

"That's great thinking on the carpet fibers," Myers said after the update. "Stay on it."

"Yes," Nellie agreed. "Please let us know as soon as you get the crime lab report."

"But I don't want to try for access to Zeke Washington's letters," Myers said. "If I know Daggett, she'll figure out you broke into Lee's apartment. Then she'd find a way to throw you both in jail. And by the way, next time you make an illegal entry, I don't need to know about it, either."

Joe and Frank exchanged smiles. They both realized that Myers wasn't exactly scolding them for getting into Lee's apartment. He was just saying he didn't want to know about it.

"What's on for tomorrow?" Frank asked.

"I'm calling some witnesses who spoke to Nick on the day of August fourteenth," Myers said. "They'll testify that Nick did not seem to be in a frame of mind that would suggest murder. Hopefully the jury will buy it. I've also got a specialist coming to point out that hair samples aren't always reliable."

"Is Nick going to testify?" Joe asked.

"I don't think it's wise," Myers said with a sigh. "I plan to wrap things up tomorrow afternoon. So if you're going to find something brilliant, it's got to be fast."

"I'll bet those carpet fibers are going to be what saves my brother," Nellie said, giving each Hardy a squeeze on the arm. "They just have to be."

"Hey, fellas, you're late!" a voice called. Joe turned to see Lisa Velloni approaching. "Listen," she said, "I need to get home so I can get to work on the day's events. Do you guys mind talking with me in my car?"

"Not unless you plan to punch us," Joe joked.

"We have to go," Frank told Nellie and Myers, "but we'll check in later tonight."

As the Hardys walked with Velloni, the reporter talked about the afternoon in court. "Sure, everyone said good things about Nick," she said, "but nothing outweighed Nellie's testimony about Nick telling Karen Lee 'sometimes I want to kill you.' That guy is going to prison."

"Don't bet on it," Frank argued.

Velloni stopped at a small car with plenty of dents and pulled a parking ticket off the windshield. "Let's go," she said, wadding up the ticket and stuffing it into her coat. Frank sat with Velloni up front, and Joe sat in back.

After starting the engine, Velloni turned on a radio. But Frank realized it was no ordinary radio. It was a scanner that picked up signals on the police radio system. There was static mixed with cross-talk between police cars and the dispatchers who tell the officers what crimes are in progress and where to go.

"I hope you don't mind," Velloni said as she drove down the street, "but I always listen to the police scanner when I drive. When a crisis occurs, I like to be one of the first to know about it."

"Why listen to music when you can have this?" Joe said. "This is better than any of those cop shows they have on TV."

"Now here's the way it works," Velloni said. "You tell me a little about your information, and then I tell you if I think it has any value to me."

The Hardys had decided they would loosen Velloni up by giving her some information, then they would try to learn some more about her. "There's a fan who's obsessed with Karen Lee," Joe said. "He writes to her, and we've seen him following her. And we think he may have something to do with the attempted murder."

"Sorry, I'm not interested," Velloni said, switching lanes to get past the heavy traffic. "Soap stars are always getting letters from crazy fans. It's no big deal. The fans are usually shy, quiet types who wouldn't hurt a fly."

"Well, I guess you're more interested in Karen Lee's side of the story," Frank said, carefully watching for Velloni's reaction. "How convenient for you that you already knew her when—"

"Shh," Velloni said, turning up the volume on the scanner.

After a moment, Velloni switched lanes again, causing several horns behind her to honk. "A fire just broke out a few blocks away," Velloni told the Hardys. "Do you mind if we make a little detour?"

"Well, I guess—" Frank began.

"I can't resist a good catastrophe," Velloni said, swinging the car into a frightening turn. "And I'll bet the fire is at one of those garment factories near Chinatown. I've been wanting to do a story on how dangerous those old places are."

Velloni turned again, driving down a street lined with twinkling lights and Italian restaurants. "Welcome to Little Italy," Velloni said. "This is where you get the best bread and pastries in town."

After a few more turns, Velloni was driving down a street with kosher butcher shops and electrical stores. Frank noticed there was Hebrew lettering in most of the windows. "Hey, watch it!" he cried as Velloni plowed through a red light.

With another turn, Velloni was driving down a narrow street in Chinatown lined with stores selling fresh fish and vegetables. When Velloni came to a truck blocking the street, she drove the car halfway onto the sidewalk, forcing several men hauling boxes to leap out of the way.

"You're as bad as the taxi drivers!" Joe yelled from the backseat.

"Worse!" Velloni said, swinging into another street lined with grimy warehouses and other buildings that looked as if they had seen much better days. A group of people was gathered near one of the buildings. Black smoke was wafting through an open door next to the fire escape on the fifth floor.

"Great, we've beaten the fire trucks," Velloni said, screeching to a stop. Then Velloni slammed out of the car. The Hardys watched her tear up the iron fire escape all the way to the fifth floor. Standing in the smoky doorway, Velloni pulled her camera from her purse and snapped a few pictures.

Then Velloni entered the building.

"She shouldn't be doing that," Frank said to Joe. "It's way too dangerous."

"Those reporters were right!" Joe exclaimed. "Lisa Velloni will do anything to get a story!"

Two minutes later, Velloni was still in the building and the fire trucks had not yet arrived. "I don't like this," Frank said, opening the car door. "We should go in after her. She might be trapped in there by the flames."

"Or it might be a trap for us," Joe said.

"What do you mean?" Frank asked.

"I'm getting bad vibes about Lunatic Lisa," Joe said. "Maybe she really did stage the attack on Lee. And maybe she now realizes we're onto her. This could be a ploy to get us inside a burning building. If we die in there, we won't be able to blow the whistle on her."

"We need to risk it anyway," Frank said, running a hand through his brown hair. "If you're wrong, Lisa Velloni may die in there. Come on."

The Hardys left the car and clambered up the fire escape to the fifth floor. They looked through the open door. Clouds of black smoke drifted through a large room jammed with huge rolls of fabric and tables with sewing machines. The overhead lights were on, but there was no one in sight.

"Lisa!" Joe called into the room. "Lisa!"

There was no answer. "Let's go," Frank said, leading Joe through the door.

The smoke curled and twisted. A smell like that of burnt toast filled the room. The Hardys both covered their mouths and noses with their coat sleeves to keep smoke from entering their lungs.

An orange glow radiated from the far end of the room. The Hardys could see the fire jumping and flickering in the hallway beyond.

"Lisa!" Joe cried out.

"Over here!" Velloni's voice called from the hallway. "Please come! I need help!"

As he moved forward, Joe wished he could see Velloni, but she was out of sight. Was it because she was trapped in the hallway by flames, or was it because she was lying in wait for the Hardys with a weapon? Either way, it was a deadly situation.

Joe's throat was dry with fear, his eyes now smarting from the swirling smoke.

Frank and Joe both knew they had no choice but to enter the smoky fire.

# 12 A Race through the Flames

The smoke grew blacker and denser as the Hardys neared the hallway. Joe coughed into his coat sleeve as he kept moving toward the fire.

"Hurry!" Velloni called.

Her voice was close. Ready to defend themselves, Frank and Joe reached the hallway.

Velloni was crouched several feet into the hallway, looking toward a room at the opposite end of it, as if searching for something. Flames were climbing the right wall near the room, devouring it with a vicious crackle. The orange-scarlet colors of the fire burned bright.

"What are you doing?" Joe cried, pulling at Velloni's coat. "We've got to get out of here!"

"We can't," Velloni protested. "I was taking

some photos through the window when I heard screams. So I came inside. There's a girl trapped in the room at the other end of this hallway."

"Hello!" Frank called.

"Help!" a female voice yelled from a room across the hall. "The fire's in here! I can't get past it." The girl sounded terrified.

Joe knew this wasn't a setup. Velloni must really be trying to help.

"She's getting weak from the smoke, and those flames are going to spread soon. We have to do something!"

Sirens wailed in the far distance.

"The fire trucks are finally coming," Frank said. "Maybe we should wait."

"They may be too late," Velloni said.

Across the hall, something exploded. The trapped girl screamed with terror.

"That explosion was probably from some kind of chemical dye," Velloni said. "That's probably how the fire began in the first place."

Frank realized Velloni was right. If they didn't do something fast, that girl might perish in the flames.

"Okay, let's get her out," Frank said, glancing around. "Joe, cut off two long pieces of fabric, the thickest you can find. You guys will throw it against the flames in the hallway, and I'll make a run for it."

A minute later, Joe and Velloni were each holding the end of a long strip of fabric. Frank closed his eyes, psyching himself up for the death-defying journey he was about to make.

There was another explosion. Opening his eyes, Frank saw a bright flash of flame across the hall.

Joe and Velloni waved the fabric against the hallway's right wall, covering as much of the flame as they could. Frank dashed through the hallway, hugging the wall on the left. Though the flames were not quite touching him, he could feel the intense heat on his hands and face.

Frank rushed into the next room. Through half of it, fire was roaring and leaping with gleeful abandon. The place was swamped with smoke and as hot as the interior of a furnace. Through stinging eyes, Frank saw a young girl crouched in a far corner, away from the flames.

"You're going to be just fine," Frank said, moving to the girl and scooping her into his arms. "Hang on." Firmly holding the girl, Frank moved to the edge of the hallway and yelled, "Go!"

Joe and Velloni threw another piece of fabric against the flames, and again Frank charged through. Frank's eyes were watering so badly he could barely see, and the heat was clawing painfully at his face, but he just kept throwing one foot in front of the other until . . .

Panting hard, Frank reached the other side and set the girl down. She was coughing and scared, but for the most part she seemed to be all right.

"The last place we were in was too cold," Joe

said, taking the girl's arm, "and this place is too hot. Come on, let's beat it!"

By the time the group reached the ground, four fire trucks, an ambulance, and a police car had arrived on the scene. Firemen with oxygen tanks on their backs barged up the fire escape while others began unrolling a giant hose from a truck.

A paramedic escorted the girl to an ambulance to see what medical care she required. Another paramedic looked over Velloni and the Hardys. In spite of the fact that their hands and faces were blackened with smoke, the paramedic found all three to be in okay condition.

"You guys have got some real guts," Velloni told the Hardys as they joined the growing crowd of people watching the action.

"We do what we have to do," Frank said modestly.

The firemen were now smashing out windows on the fifth floor to let the heat escape. As Velloni's red hair blew in the wind, it reminded Frank of the leaping flames he had just seen.

"So that *was* you in Nick's apartment," Frank blurted out suddenly. "And on the rooftop, too."

"We've just risked our lives together," Velloni said. "I think we can be honest with each other now. Yes, I broke into Rodriguez's apartment last night. Picked the lock. When you two came in,

114

I hid behind a couch. Then I ran up to the roof."

"Why were you in Nick's place?" Joe asked.

"I have access to Karen Lee for information on this case," Velloni explained. "But Nick and his family are refusing to talk with me. So I wanted to see what I could find on Nick. And I'll bet you guys were there for the same reason."

"So why did you knock my brother off the roof?" Joe said, giving Velloni a light shove.

"I . . . I didn't," Velloni said, surprised.

"You knocked me off the roof," Frank stated.

"What?" Velloni said, looking bewildered. "I just meant to knock you down so you wouldn't follow me. Then I ran to get out of there. I had no idea I knocked you over the edge. If there's any way I can make it up to you, let me know."

"You can tell me something," Frank said. "Do you have a carpet or rug in your apartment?"

"No, I don't," Velloni said, looking confused. "Why?"

"No reason," Frank said with a shrug.

"Well, fellas," Velloni said, pulling a tape recorder from her large purse, "if you'll excuse me, I want to interview the little girl we just rescued. I wonder if she had just been on the premises with someone or if she actually worked here. I might be able to get a really important story out of it!"

Joe watched Velloni hurry to a cluster of women standing near the ambulance. "The fact that she would risk her life to save that girl makes it seem less likely she's our culprit," he said, scratching his head. "I just wish we could have gotten some carpet fibers from her."

"We did," Frank said, pulling a packet from his coat. "I got some from the carpet in her car, and I get the impression she spends a lot of time there. We've got samples now from three suspects."

"Great," Joe said, noticing how smoke-blackened his hands were. "Now we just need some good soap."

Several hours later, a cleaner Frank and Joe were walking along Fifth Avenue, looking at the elaborate Christmas displays in the store windows. Overhead, white holiday lights glimmered the length of the entire street. The night air was sharp, but a good many people were out strolling, many carrying shopping bags.

"That was a great steak dinner," Joe said.

"Best I've had in a while," Frank agreed.

Right after the fire, the Hardys had taken all the fiber samples to Sergeant Tyrell, who said he would send them to the crime lab and would have a report, probably before nine that night. Frank and Joe had decided to stay in the city. If the fibers from one of their suspects matched up, they wanted to pay a visit to that particular suspect immediately.

"Maybe you should have gotten Callie one of

116

these," Joe said. He was pointing at the window display of one of the world's most famous jewelry stores. Several luminous diamond rings were resting on a drape of red velvet.

"No problem," Frank said. "These probably don't cost much more than our family's house."

As the Hardys resumed walking, Frank checked his watch. It was ten past nine. Frank's stomach was jittery. So far none of the leads he and Joe had followed had turned into anything definite. That meant everything depended on the fibers Sergeant Tyrell was late calling about.

As he passed the spectacular structure of St. Patrick's Cathedral, Frank found himself wondering about the other article of evidence he had seen, the tiny piece of pink enamel. What was it? And did it have anything to do with the attempted murder? Frank still could not imagine what the object was.

"Cool," Joe said as he and Frank came to the plaza at Rockefeller Center. A crowd of people were looking down on a vast skating rink, filled with people skimming across the ice.

"That's an amazing tree," Frank commented. In front of a skyscraper across the rink, a huge Christmas tree soared seven stories high, decorated with brightly colored lights and ornaments.

The Hardys both leaned on a railing to admire the holiday scene, but Joe could see his brother's

117

mind was elsewhere. "You still think Nick is innocent, don't you?" Joe said.

"Yes, I do," Frank said, his eyes on the skaters. "Do you still think he's guilty?"

"After everything that's happened today," Joe said, "I'm afraid I still think he's guilty. But I'm also seeing how important it is for a person to have the best possible defense."

"Why is that?" Frank asked.

"I had moments this afternoon," Joe said, "when I considered each one of our suspects guilty—John Q., Alex, Velloni. But obviously that can't be the case. I guess a fair trial is the best way to keep a jury from making that kind of mistake."

"And then sometimes a jury makes the wrong decision even if the trial is fair," Frank said.

Joe watched a skater wipe out on the ice. "Do you really think they'll convict Nick?" Joe asked.

Frank nodded. "Unless we can come up with something linking someone else to the crime, Nick Rodriguez is going to spend this Christmas and a lot of others behind bars. And the thought of that really bothers me. But so far we've got nothing.

"Let's go call Tyrell," he said. As he and Joe went to find a pay phone, Frank's stomach churned. He knew that what he was about to find out could either set Nick Rodriguez free or send him to jail for many years to come.

# 13 Sing Sing

"Hello." Frank spoke into the phone, his heart pounding.

"Hi, Frank," the voice of Sergeant Tyrell returned. "Listen, I just got the call from the crime lab. None of the fibers you brought in matches those found at the crime scene. Sorry, but that's how it goes in the detective game. You win some and you lose some."

"Yeah," Frank said, his heart sinking. "But I really appreciate the help."

"It really wasn't much trouble," Tyrell said. "Say hello to your dad for me."

"I sure will," Frank replied.

As Frank hung up the phone, Joe could read the bad news in his brother's face. In fact, Frank looked as down as Joe had ever seen him. "Frank, we did our best," Joe said gently.

The two brothers walked back to the rink. Frank leaned on the railing and watched the skaters gliding across the ice. Some were graceful, and some were clumsy. At the moment, Frank felt a lot like the ones who were falling roughly to the ice. "I just wish I knew what to do," he said wearily.

He stared at the ice a long moment.

"Maybe there's one more thing," he said.

"What's that?" Joe asked.

"I keep hearing the voice of Zeke Washington saying, 'In the name of justice, I have to talk to you,' " Frank said. "I think we should go to Sing Sing tomorrow morning and see what he was talking about. It may be nothing, but it's worth a shot."

"Okay," Joe said with a nod. "We're there."

"Well," Frank said, casting a last look at the gigantic tree, "let's head back to Bayport and get some rest. Besides, I've got to give Callie her present tonight."

At ten-thirty the following morning, the Hardys walked toward the prison after an hour's train ride from Manhattan. They had learned the train stopped right near the prison grounds and figured it would be faster than driving from Bayport in the van.

After passing through several gates, several

120

guards, and several heavy doors, the Hardys spoke with a prison official, who made the necessary arrangements for the Hardys to speak with inmate 82658—Zeke Washington.

The Hardys were brought into a large room that was divided in half by a wall of bulletproof glass. Prisoners sat on one side of the glass, visitors on the other. All around, people were conversing with their friends and loved ones who were serving time at the prison. Like everything else at Sing Sing, the room was drab and depressing.

Soon a young man came to sit across the glass from Frank and Joe. He picked up a telephone to speak with the Hardys, both of whom also picked up phones. "I'm Zeke Washington," the man spoke into his mouthpiece. "I understand you want to see me."

Zeke wore a light blue shirt with his prisoner number printed over the pocket. Joe had expected to see a hardened criminal. Instead he was face-to-face with a pleasant man only a few years older than himself. Except for the prison attire, Zeke could have been a buddy from Bayport High.

"We understand you have some information for Karen Lee," Frank said.

"Well, you see," Zeke Washington said, "I need Karen Lee to help me get out of here."

"How is that?" Joe asked.

"I've been a criminal most of my life, and I

admit that," Zeke said. "I robbed a bunch of places, and I've been in and out of prison more times than I can count. Fact is, a lot of folks call me Elmer because they used to say my hands were as sticky as glue."

Zeke showed a charming smile. Joe found himself liking this man, even though, in a sense, he played for the opposite team.

"But, you see," Zeke continued, "a year and a half ago I gave up crime for good. Even got myself a real job."

"Then why are you here?" Joe asked.

"Good question," Zeke said, turning more serious. "Right after I went straight, I got arrested on an armed robbery charge. They said I held up the clerk of a convenience store at gunpoint. I was convicted of the crime and sentenced to fifteen years. I've been here for eight months already. But I didn't do the crime."

Frank tapped his foot impatiently. None of this seemed important to Nick's trial.

"I have a lot of free time here," Zeke continued. "Instead of just playing cards and watching TV like most of the other inmates, I decided to find out what went wrong in my case and see if there was anything I could do about it."

"That was smart," Joe told Zeke.

"I read some law books and wrote a lot of letters," Zeke said. "Then, last August, I tracked down and called the police detective who worked my case, a Detective O'Roark. He told me he found the gun that I supposedly used in the armed robbery. He traced the serial number and found it belonged to someone else, another guy known for being a crook."

"Was that information admitted at your trial?" Frank asked, checking his watch.

"It should have been, but it wasn't," Zeke said. "One day last spring, right before my trial started, O'Roark brought this information to the lawyer prosecuting the case. He said this proved my innocence and they should go after the other guy instead. But the prosecutor ignored this information. The other guy had skipped town, and the prosecutor wanted a quick victory."

"In other words," Joe said, "the prosecutor withheld crucial evidence. Which is illegal."

"That's exactly what she did," Zeke said.

"What was the prosecutor's name?" Frank asked.

"Patricia Daggett," Zeke said, mouthing the words as if they left a bad taste in his mouth.

Frank and Joe looked at each other. "I think she has a reputation for that," Joe told Zeke.

"That's what Detective O'Roark told me," Zeke said. "He told me he knew of several other times where Daggett withheld evidence to win a case. Just minor things here and there. None of them as bad as what she did to me."

Frank did not know where this was leading, but he was getting the impression this visit had been a wise move. "What does this have to do with

Karen Lee?" Frank asked, his brown eyes studying Zeke.

"I'm planning to file a complaint with the head district attorney that states Patricia Daggett railroaded me into jail," Zeke said. "O'Roark told me he had a big argument with Daggett that day last spring when he realized she wasn't going to use the evidence he had uncovered. I asked O'Roark if anyone overheard their argument, and he told me there was a secretary nearby."

Frank now realized where this was going. "And after some more digging," Frank said, "you discovered that secretary was named Karen Lee. And you figured if Lee could back up O'Roark's story, the head DA might believe it."

"Man, you're reading my thoughts," Zeke said, leaning forward. "But by this time, Lee had left her secretary job and was acting on some soap opera. Her address and phone number were unlisted, so I wrote several letters to her at the television studio where she works. I explained the situation to her and told her how she could contact me."

"But she didn't answer the letters," Joe said.

"No," Zeke said, shaking his head. "Finally I got smart and found her home phone number in last year's phone book. I called her yesterday and left a message. But she hasn't gotten back to me."

"Are you aware that Karen Lee is mixed up in a trial of her own?" Frank asked. "I think it's been a big story in some of the tabloids."

"I don't read that stuff," Zeke said. "What's she on trial for? Bad acting?"

Joe laughed and then explained the circumstances surrounding Karen Lee's trial.

"I see," Zeke said when the explanation was done. "So Miss Lee has probably been too busy to care about my letters."

Zeke lowered his head. A sense of doom seemed to have fallen on him. Joe could imagine what he was thinking—a soap opera star with big problems of her own would probably never have time to help some poor guy sitting in a prison fifty miles away.

"It's not so hopeless," Joe told Zeke. "Your letters were just mixed up with all her other fan letters. She's a decent person, and maybe she *will* care if she learns how important your letters are."

"Do you think," Zeke said, finally looking up, "you could maybe explain things to her? If she can verify Detective O'Roark's story, I feel sure the head district attorney will see that Patricia Daggett has been abusing the legal system. I hate to trouble you guys, but . . . I'm afraid Karen Lee is my only chance of getting out of here."

"Zeke, we can't promise anything," Joe said, placing a hand against the glass, "but we'll do whatever we can to help you."

"I would really appreciate that," Zeke said.

Joe and Zeke talked a little more, but Frank had fallen silent. Then a guard came over and tapped Zeke on the shoulder. Goodbyes were said, then Zeke and the Hardys set down their phones.

Frank now had his hands over his face. He was deep in thought, totally unaware of all the conversations taking place in the visiting room. Finally Frank looked at Joe.

"What's on your mind?" Joe asked.

"I believe Zeke is telling the truth," Frank replied. "Do you know what that could mean?"

"What?" Joe said, dying to know.

"It could mean," Frank said in a quiet tone, "that Patricia Daggett is the one who tried to murder Karen Lee."

# 14 Dark at the End of the Tunnel

The Hardys wasted no time catching the next train back to Manhattan. As they took seats in a half-empty car, the train left the station.

Joe glanced out the window at the peaceful scenery passing by. Clouds drifted through a blue sky, and the rolling green water of the Hudson River followed the train tracks. Across the river, low hills stretched along the shore.

"I'm ready," Frank said, turning to Joe. He had barely spoken since the Hardys left the prison visiting room. While Joe patiently waited, Frank had been carefully thinking matters through.

"Okay," Joe said. "Let's put this together, piece by piece. I'm still not sure I see how and why Patricia Daggett tried to kill Karen Lee."

"Remember, Bernie said Daggett makes it her business to know everything."

"Yeah," Joe said, nodding.

"Chances are," Frank continued, "last August she found out Zeke had contacted Detective O'Roark. A man who knew she withheld crucial evidence from Zeke's trial."

"Then what?" Joe asked. "Did Daggett discover Zeke had also tracked down the name of Karen Lee?"

"Exactly," Frank said. "Lee probably wasn't aware that Daggett was withholding evidence. She probably still isn't aware of it. But if she heard the argument between O'Roark and Daggett, she would be able to back up O'Roark's story."

"In other words, Zeke was right," Joe said. "Karen Lee is the one person who could make the head district attorney believe that Daggett has been abusing the legal system."

"If word of this got out," Frank said, "it would destroy Daggett's legal career. Not to mention her dream to be elected district attorney."

"But is she so ambitious," Joe wondered aloud, "that she would try to kill Karen Lee just to protect her own reputation?"

"As we've seen many times," Frank said, "there's no telling what people are capable of."

"Okay, we've got the why," Joe said. "Let's move on to the how."

128

"It could have worked like this," Frank said, focusing his thoughts. "On the night of August fourteenth, Daggett went to Karen Lee's apartment building. She probably entered the building, unnoticed, when someone came in or went out. Like we did with the postman. Then she climbed the steps to the third floor and put on a black coat, black gloves, and a black ski mask."

"Then through the window in the stairwell door," Joe picked up, "she saw Nick leaving the apartment. That was the face Nick told us he saw. Daggett couldn't have known Nick would be there, so that must have been a stroke of good luck for her."

"Right after Nick got on the elevator," Frank continued, "Daggett knocked at Lee's door. When Lee opened the door, Daggett barged in and pulled out a knife. She tried to kill Lee, but she's not experienced at this type of thing. Lee managed to fight her off, and Daggett fled the scene."

"So you think she framed Nick?" Joe asked.

"I think she did. Very soon after the attack," Frank replied, "Daggett began to worry that the crime might somehow get traced back to her, maybe through Zeke. But she realized if she could successfully frame someone else, she'd never be suspected of the crime."

"Immediately she thought of Nick Rodriguez," Joe said. "Most likely she knew about his relationship with Lee, and she probably even knew he was angry at Lee for breaking off the engagement. And, best of all, he was at Lee's apartment right before the murder attempt. He was the perfect suspect!"

"She thinks Lee may have a set of keys to Nick's apartment," Frank said, more and more excited as he spoke. "So the next day, while Lee is out, Daggett climbs the fire escape and goes through an open window into Lee's apartment. She finds the keys to Nick's place. Remember, they had Nick's first name on them."

"Then, using the stolen keys," Joe said, "she gets into Nick's apartment while he's away at work. She brings the gloves and ski mask with her."

"Except they're probably a *different* pair of gloves and ski mask that look just like the ones she used for the attack," Frank said. "That way there won't be any traces of her own hair on them."

"She gets some hair from Nick's comb or brush and puts it in the ski mask," Joe said. "Then she stuffs the gloves and mask under Nick's mattress."

"The cops had examined Nick's place the night before," Frank said, "but Daggett, who would have already jumped into the case, convinces them to check again. The next day the cops find the gloves and mask. Nick looks guilty as sin, the cops arrest him, and he goes to trial for the murder attempt."

"It all fits!" Joe said, pounding the seat in front of him. "It fits perfectly!"

"Well, it *could* have happened that way," Frank said, placing a hand on Joe's shoulder. "However, we have no absolute proof it *did* happen that way."

"You know," Joe said, calming down, "on second thought, I'm not thrilled about accusing an assistant district attorney of attempted murder. If we're wrong, we'll look ridiculous. And if we're right, she's in a position to make things very difficult for us. To save her reputation, she might find a way to put *us* in jail. She's probably smart enough to do it."

"I know," Frank said, rubbing his face. "I wish we had some solid proof to back up our story. So far we're still in the realm of guesswork."

"What should we do?" Joe asked.

"Let's get to the courthouse as soon as possible and talk to Bernie," Frank said, stretching his legs as the train rushed onward.

At one-thirty, the train came to a stop at Grand Central Terminal in Manhattan. The Hardys hurried through a door and found the subway.

After descending two flights of steps, the Hardys paid their fare and headed for the platform. Frank drummed his fingers on his pants, waiting for the train that would take the Hardys downtown.

Then Frank noticed a man near the end of the platform, reading a tabloid newspaper. The tabloid's cover showed a photograph of a space alien with its arms around a famous country music star. Then Frank noticed the man behind the paper also looked pretty strange.

It was the man with the red-green hair.

"Look," Frank said, tugging Joe's arm. "It's that guy from the park. This could be a chance to find out if Daggett sent this guy to do her dirty work."

"Let's go," Joe said, already in motion.

The man with the red-green hair turned to see the Hardys approaching. Dropping the paper, he hurried to the very edge of the platform—then leaped off into the train pit. Amazed, Joe watched the man run along the tracks, quickly disappearing into the darkness of the tunnel.

"Should we go after him?" Joe asked.

"Oh, why not?" Frank replied sarcastically. "Compared to leaping into a burning building, this is nothing."

Frank and Joe lowered themselves into the train pit, then began running along the tracks. Darkness surrounded them, and they heard their footsteps echoing in the cavernous space. They also heard footsteps clattering in the distance ahead.

"Watch out for the third rail!" Frank called to Joe. Both Hardys knew the thick railing that ran parallel to the train tracks carried the electricity that powered the trains.

"No problem!" Joe called back.

Then, as if he were back on the football field at Bayport High, Joe put on a burst of speed. He rushed past steel beams and electrical cables, gaining on the fleeing footsteps ahead. Taking a flying leap, Joe seized the man by his coat and said, "Hey, buddy, I'd like to finish that conversation we started yesterday!"

The man spun around, and Joe could see the guy's pocketknife. With a flick, the long blade shot out. The man lunged with the blade at Joe's face.

"I don't think so," Frank said, grabbing the man's wrist before the blade could reach Joe. Twisting the man's wrist, Frank said, "Drop it!"

"Ahhh!" the man cried in pain, letting the knife fall to the tracks.

All three of them were panting now. "Do you know what that is?" Joe said, jerking the man's head toward the dangerous third rail.

"Yeah, I know what it is," the man said. "If you touch it, you get fried like a piece of bacon."

"Well, that's what's going to happen to you," Joe said roughly, "unless you do some talking."

The man's eyes glared like a creature with rabies, but he seemed to get the point. "How can I be of help to you boys?" he spat out.

"Who sent you after us?" Frank asked.

The man hesitated, then spoke. "Some lawyer in the DA's office," he said. "Daggett or somebody."

"You're doing real well," Joe said, still holding the man. "Now, how do you know Daggett?"

Frank glanced up the tunnel toward the station. He realized this would be a very inconvenient time for a train to come. This interview needed to be real fast.

"I'm scheduled to go on trial for burglary in a few weeks," the man explained. "Daggett is prosecuting the case. Yesterday morning she called me up and said she'd go easy on me in court if I'd do her a small favor. She wanted me to scare you away from whatever you were investigating."

Frank recalled seeing Daggett on a pay phone at the courthouse the day before, immediately after she met the Hardys. Shortly after that, Frank realized, the man with the red-green hair had appeared in the park.

"When Bernie filed the motion for us to view the evidence," Frank told Joe, "Daggett knew we were on the case. When she met us, she figured out we were the ones who learned about the missing keys. Because that's another example of withholding evidence, it must have made her nervous."

"Look, I don't have any idea what this business is about, and I don't care," the man said, itchy to get away. "It's nothing personal. I was just trying to save my own skin."

"We're touched," Joe said.

"Watch it!" the man cried, pointing to the ground. Joe jumped, seeing a gigantic rat scurry over the tracks straight for his shoes.

In a flash, the man pulled free of Joe. He tore down the tracks, yelling, "Sorry, fellas, just remembered I'm late for a very important appointment!"

Joe started after the man, but Frank grabbed his arm. "I hate it when you do this!" Joe yelled.

"Let him go!" Frank yelled back. "Now we know for sure Daggett's the one we want."

"But we still don't have any hard evidence!" Joe protested. "That's why we need that creep."

"No," Frank argued. "Even if we could haul that jerk into court, no one would believe him."

A rumbling sound made both Hardys whip around.

Two beams of light pierced the tunnel.

"The train is coming!" Joe exclaimed. "We didn't hear it pull in!"

"And now it's pulling out," Frank said.

The train's engine rumbled as it accelerated out of the station. Like the eyes of an approaching monster, the headlights grew larger and larger.

"Hey!" Joe yelled, waving his arms at the train. "Stop! We're standing on the track!"

"Stop!" Frank called out. "Stop! Stop!"

Frank saw a driver through a window in the train's front car, but the driver did not seem to see the Hardys. Frank glanced at the concrete walls on either side. The tunnel was just wide enough for the train, leaving no extra room for the Hardys to escape its path.

The train was now picking up speed.

"He doesn't see us!" Joe yelled frantically.

"Only one thing to do!" Frank shouted. "Run!"

# 15 The Whole Truth

Frank and Joe dashed down the tracks, away from the approaching train.

"Yesterday I saw men working on the tracks!" Joe yelled over the train's engine. "There must be a safe place they go when a train comes through!"

"This would be a great time to find it!" Frank called back.

Running with all his might, Frank felt the ground vibrating under his feet, and it seemed his heart was slamming against the wall of his chest. The train's rumble was now echoing nightmarishly loud in the tunnel.

Headlights flooded the Hardy's path, but the driver still was not slowing or stopping the train. It seemed the train was almost up to full speed.

Frank could sense the train breathing down his back, just about to crush him. He figured he and Joe had about three seconds left.

"Against the wall on the right!" Joe yelled.

By the light of the train, Frank saw several man-size indentations in the tunnel's wall. Frank realized that must be where the repairmen went.

Frank and Joe both dived up against one of the indentations. They froze, still as statues.

A second later, the train roared by, the cars rattling on the tracks with a deafening racket. The silver train was only inches from the Hardys, but that was enough to save their lives. Seconds later the train was speeding away, showing only two red lights on the rear car.

"Good news and bad news," Joe said as the train's din faded. "We didn't get demolished by that train, but now we have to wait for the next one."

"I wonder what happened to our friend," Frank said, looking down the tunnel. "Even though he's not my favorite person, I kind of hope he's okay."

After catching their breath, Frank and Joe returned to the platform. Only a few of the waiting passengers glanced their way, as if the sight of two well-dressed young men emerging from the tunnel was an everyday occurrence. Minutes later they caught another train downtown.

When they reached the criminal court building, the trial was just about to resume after the lunchtime break. The Hardys huddled with Myers and Nick at the defense table and hurriedly explained everything they had learned that day.

"This is incredible," Myers said, pulling a pencil from behind his ear. "Just incredible."

"But it makes perfect sense," Nick said, gripping Myers on the arm. "We have to use it!"

"Unfortunately," Myers said, "all the information Frank and Joe have collected today is just hearsay. That means it came from conversations neither of them was actually present for."

"Which means it's not allowed in court," Joe grumbled.

Frank watched Daggett take a seat at her table. She appeared to be perfectly composed, from the top of her frosted blond hair to her shiny high heels.

"But . . ." Myers said, twirling the pencil in his hand, "maybe there's a way for me to attack Daggett and still play by the rules. I may not be able to show that she's the one who attempted the murder. But there's a chance I can show how she's made Nick's trial extremely unfair."

As the courtroom filled with people, Myers, Nick, and the Hardys spent a few frenzied minutes coming up with a plan. When the judge entered and called the trial back into session, Myers explained that, based on some new information, he wanted to call a few unexpected witnesses. The judge agreed.

Then Myers called Joe Hardy to the witness stand. The crowd watched with interest as Joe explained that he and Frank were working as PIs for the defense. Then Myers got to the point. "Mr. Hardy," Myers said, "did you and your brother speak with Karen Lee on Monday of this week?"

"Yes, we did," Joe replied.

"And did you ask her about a certain set of keys?" Myers asked.

"That's correct," Joe said. "We asked if she had the keys to Nick Rodriguez's apartment. She said she did. However, shortly after the attempted murder, she noticed the keys were missing."

"I see," Myers said, turning to face the jury. "Well, that could be very significant to this case, as it indicates someone may have stolen those keys so they could plant the gloves and ski mask in Mr. Rodriguez's apartment. By any chance did Miss Lee indicate to you that she had informed Miss Daggett of the missing keys?"

"Objection," Daggett said calmly.

"Your Honor," Myers told the judge, "I am establishing that Miss Daggett may have withheld crucial information in her zeal to convict the defendant."

"Objection overruled," the judge declared. "You may answer the question, Mr. Hardy."

"Karen Lee told us," Joe said, "she had informed Miss Daggett about the missing keys."

"That'll be all," Myers said, smiling at Joe.

"I have no cross-examination, Your Honor," Daggett said from her table. She was only several feet away, and Frank was watching her closely. In spite of Joe's testimony, she seemed remarkably cool, maybe showing just a tiny bit of nervousness by the way she twirled her flower ring.

Next Myers called Karen Lee to the witness stand. He asked if she had overheard the argument between Daggett and Detective O'Roark. Lee did remember the argument. She even remembered a discussion about the serial number of a gun and O'Roark accusing Daggett of withholding evidence.

In spite of numerous objections from Daggett, Lee was able to continue with this testimony.

"Myers is playing this well," Joe told Frank. "Lee's testimony combined with mine is showing how Daggett plays with the legal system. This could give the jury some serious doubt about convicting Nick, don't you think?"

Frank nodded, but he wasn't sure. If Nick was to go free, the jury needed some real proof. Guesswork wasn't enough, he noted sadly, even though it was obvious that Daggett was the one who attacked Karen Lee.

Finished with Lee, Myers returned to his seat. Frank kept his eyes on Daggett as she cross-examined Lee from her table. Frank had to hand it to the woman. Except for a little bit of ring twirling, she was still as cool as an ice cube.

Then Frank's eyes focused like a laser on the ring. One of the petals was missing. The missing part was just a tiny piece of painted enamel, but right now it was the biggest thing in the world to Frank.

Frank realized the missing petal was the piece of pink enamel he had seen in the evidence room. The shape was exactly the same as the other petals.

That's it, Frank thought—the petal is the proof!

Frank scrawled out a note and quickly passed it to Myers. "This better be good," Myers wrote back.

When the cross-examination was done, a very confused Myers asked the judge for a one-hour break in the trial, and the judge agreed.

During the break, Frank explained what he had discovered, and Myers arranged to have the piece of pink enamel brought over from the evidence room. Daggett did not try to block this move, and Frank realized she did not yet understand what the all-important piece of pink enamel was.

When the trial resumed, Myers called Frank to the witness stand. "Mr. Hardy," Myers said, hands casually in his pockets, "yesterday, did you examine the physical evidence connected to this case?"

"Yes, I did," Frank answered.

Myers picked up the plastic packet containing the piece of pink enamel and showed it to the members of the jury. Then he showed it to Frank and asked, "Was this one of the things you saw there?"

"Yes, it was," Frank said.

"What is it?" Myers asked.

"It's a piece of painted enamel that was found at the crime scene," Frank explained. "Since Karen Lee had swept her floor shortly before the attack and since the police retrieved this item shortly after the attack, it is believed to have fallen to the ground sometime around the time of the murder attempt. No one at the crime lab knew what it was, but a short while ago I figured it out."

"And what is this little item?" Myers asked.

"It's a flower petal from a ring," Frank said.

"I'm confused," Myers said, removing his glasses. "This is just a tiny piece of pink enamel. How can you be certain it's a petal from a ring?"

"Because," Frank said, his eyes drifting toward the prosecutor, "this exact petal is missing from the ring that Patricia Daggett is now wearing on the index finger of her right hand."

Gasps of amazement were heard throughout the room. The judge pounded his gavel.

"That's all," Myers said, taking a seat.

Frank knew Myers could not get him to say Daggett was the culprit because Frank had not actually witnessed the attack. But maybe some of the jury members were putting everything together and seeing how the petal proved Daggett's guilt. And maybe Frank could somehow drive the point a little more on the cross-examination.

Daggett stood, her eyes glinting like daggers.

"Mr. Hardy," Daggett said evenly, "you are a very observant boy. Indeed, I am wearing a flower ring with painted enamel petals. And, yes, one of those petals is missing. But what on earth makes you think the petal found at the crime scene came from my ring?"

Daggett was staring straight at Frank, daring him to accuse her, a respected and powerful lawyer, of the crime in question. Frank was in a dangerous position, and Daggett was obviously hoping he would back down. But Frank was not in the mood for backing down today.

"I know it came from your ring," Frank said, acting every bit as cool as Daggett, "because you were the person who tried to murder Karen Lee."

The courtroom went dead silent.

Then came the clicking of Daggett's high heels as she slowly approached the witness stand. Again she reminded Frank of a spider spinning a web. "May I ask your age?" Daggett said to Frank.

"Objection!" Myers cried out.

"Overruled," the judge declared.

"I am eighteen years old," Frank replied.

"Let me offer another theory," Daggett said, giving Frank the sweetest of smiles. "Perhaps you and your brother are a pair of teenagers pretending to be detectives, and you are terribly determined to prove to all of us adults just how clever you are. Even though you don't have the slightest idea what you are talking about. Who knows? Perhaps your parents don't pay enough attention to you."

Frank knew what Daggett was doing. Her scare tactics had failed, so now she was trying to make Frank seem immature to the jury.

"We *are* detectives," Frank said in his most professional tone. "And our parents give us plenty of attention."

Daggett twirled her ring and then stopped herself. Frank could see she was thinking up a new line of questioning.

"Let me ask you this," Daggett said. "If I was the one who attacked Karen Lee that night, then would I not have been wearing gloves at the time?"

"You *were* wearing gloves," Frank said.

"Then how could the petal from the ring have found its way to the floor?" Daggett asked.

Frank realized Daggett was now trying to trip him up on details. But Frank had already considered this particular detail.

"As Miss Lee stated in her testimony," Frank said, "she grabbed the attacker's right hand. The hand with the knife and also the ring. Karen Lee said she held the hand tightly, struggling with it. Under those conditions, the petal could easily have broken off and slipped through the glove."

Daggett turned to the jury, chuckling and shaking her head in disbelief. "Well, Mr. Hardy," she remarked, "it seems you're quite the crime scene expert, doesn't it? I wouldn't be surprised if you have your own junior detective kit in your toy chest at home!"

Frank knew it was time for the kill.

"The jury shouldn't have to take my word for this," Frank said, loud and clear. "Perhaps you would allow a reenactment of the struggle to be staged with a similar ring. I believe this will prove my theory to be correct. Then perhaps the jury will finally have 'the whole truth and nothing but the truth' about who it was who really tried to murder Karen Lee on the night of August fourteenth!"

The crowd went wild with excitement, and it took the judge a full minute to get everyone quiet.

"All right," the judge announced when order had been finally restored. "In view of the most unusual accusations being made, I am ending this trial for the day. I would like to see both lawyers in my private chamber at once. Court is dismissed!"

The judge banged his gavel.

At ten the following morning, Frank and Joe were standing on the steps of the criminal court building. After meeting with the lawyers the day before, the judge had spent the rest of the day and much of the night examining the case in light of the new revelations. The trial was still on hold, and the judge was now meeting with both lawyers again.

It was cold out, but the sky was a brilliant blue. "Well," Joe said, a breath of fog coming from his mouth, "either we're going to be in big demand as private investigators for criminal trials, or we're going to spend this Christmas in jail."

A few minutes later, three people walked out of the court building—Myers, Nellie, and Nick.

"Nick," Frank said, surprised. "You're out!"

"After considering everything," Nick said with a smile, "the judge dismissed the case against me."

"And he had Patricia Daggett arrested for the attempted murder of Karen Lee and about fifty other charges," Nellie explained.

"She's plenty mad at you guys," Myers added.

"I'll bet she is," Joe said.

"Frank, Joe," Nick said, placing a hand on

147

each of the brothers, "I can't even begin to thank you."

"Because of you two," Nellie said with a look of deep appreciation, "justice has been done."

Then someone else was standing nearby— Karen Lee. She approached the group and gently touched the arm of Nick's coat. "I'm sorry," she said in a soft voice. "I should have known you would never try to kill me. But there was so much evidence against you, and Miss Daggett was so persuasive that I . . ."

"As long as you believe me now," Nick said.

"As soon as we pick up Nick's things at the jail," Myers told the Hardys, "we're having a celebration, and we insist you guys come."

"And you, too, Karen," Nick said.

"I'd be honored," Karen told Nick.

"Count us in," Joe said happily.

Myers, Lee, Nellie, and Nick headed for the House of Detention, promising to come back for the Hardys when they were done there. Frank looked back at the grimy court building and noticed the engraved words: Justice Denied No One.

"Man, oh man," Joe told Frank. "You've got quite a report to make to your civics class."

"And you know something?" Frank said. "I think we may have some more business here."

"Why is that?" Joe asked.

"It sounds as if Patricia Daggett is in some

pretty hot water," Frank explained. "I was thinking she might need a good team of teenage PIs. After all, everyone is entitled to a fair trial."

"True," Joe said with a gleam in his eye. "But do you think we might be able to raise our rates this time?"

# BRAND-NEW SERIES!

## Meet up with suspense and mystery in

## #1 The Gross Ghost Mystery

Frank and Joe are making friends and meeting monsters!

## #2 The Karate Clue

Somebody's kicking up a major mess!

## #3 First Day, Worst Day

Everybody's mad at Joe! Is he a tattletale?

## By Franklin W. Dixon

Look for a brand-new story every other month
at your local bookseller

A MINSTREL® BOOK

Published by Pocket Books          1398-01

# NANCY DREW® MYSTERY STORIES  By Carolyn Keene

A MINSTREL® BOOK
## Published by Pocket Books

Simon & Schuster, Mail Order Dept. HB5, 200 Old Tappan Rd., Old Tappan, N.J. 07675
Please send me copies of the books checked. Please add appropriate local sales tax.
☐ Enclosed full amount per copy with this coupon (Send check or money order only)
☐ If order is $10.00 or more, you may charge to one of the following accounts:  ☐ Mastercard  ☐ Visa
Please be sure to include proper postage and handling: 0.95 for first copy; 0.50 for each additional copy ordered.
Name _____
Address _____
City _____  State/Zip _____
Credit Card # _____  Exp.Date _____
Signature _____
Books listed are also available at your bookstore.  Prices are subject to change without notice.

760-27